אוניסטה

פרוב׳אד׳ה פיר סו מ׳ארידו

קומפואיסטו

פול: אליה ר. קארמונה

דיריקטור דיל ג׳וג׳יטון

קונסטאנטינופלה

5685

אימפרימיריאה »סוחוליט«

Benjamin B Joseph — Libraire

Stamboul Barnathan Han = Constantinople

Portada de la edición original de
La Mužer Onesta.

Title page of the first edition of
La Mužer Onesta.

The
Chaste
Wife

The Chaste Wife
(La Muz'er Onesta)

Elia R Karmona

Translated and introduced by
Michael Alpert

Five Leaves
<u>www.fiveleaves.co.uk</u>

The Chaste Wife *by Elia R Karmona*

was first published in Ladino
as *La Muz'er Onesta*
by Benjamin B. Joseph,
Constantinople 1924/5 (5685)
in Hebrew type

This edition published in 2009
by Five Leaves
PO Box 8786, Nottingham NG1 9AW
www.fiveleaves.co.uk

ISBN: 978 1 905512 66 9

Five Leaves acknowledges financial support
from Arts Council England

Five Leaves is a member of Inpress
(www.inpressbooks.co.uk),
representing independent publishers

Cover design: Darius Hinks
Typesetting and layout: Four Sheets
Printed in Great Britain

Contents

Preface

In 1492, the Inquisition persuaded the rulers of Spain to expel those Jews who after a century of pressure were still reluctant to accept Christian baptism. Tens of thousands of them were expelled from the land where their ancestors had lived for over one thousand years, and many emigrated to the Ottoman Empire, which in 1453 had captured Constantinople and was still expanding.

Over the following centuries they were followed by other Spanish Jews who had gone first to Italy, Portugal or North Africa. They settled in cities of the Ottoman Empire such as Belgrade, Sarajevo, Sofia, Salonika, Constantinople, Smyrna, Aleppo, Safed, Tiberias, Jerusalem, Hebron, Cairo and Alexandria. They kept their Spanish practices and language. At its height, in the mid-XIXth century, the population of Spanish-speaking Jews in the Ottoman Empire reached 300,000.

From then onward, emigration — mainly to Western Europe and North and South America — began to reduce the Spanish-speaking Jewish population of the Middle East. Later, in the countries which emerged as independent nations after the collapse of the Turkish Empire in 1918, powerful nationalism tended to absorb Jewish culture. In the war of 1939-1945, the German occupation of the Balkans, Greece and the island of Rhodes, followed by deportation and the mass murder of Jews, completed the destruction of those centuries-old communities.

After the war, most of the survivors moved to Western Europe and the New World, while the establishment of the State of Israel in 1948 added substantial numbers to the long-existing population of Spanish-speaking Jews in Palestine.

The Spanish language of 1492, with its natural changes over the years and the adoption of many Turkish and Greek words, was the language spoken, written and

9

read by the Spanish or Sephardi* Jews. However, the growth of local nationalisms after the collapse of the multilingual Ottoman Empire in 1918, together with emigration, as well as the powerful influence of French on the two or three generations of Sephardi Jews who were educated in the schools of the *Alliance Israélite Internationale*, were by the 1930s already weakening the use of Spanish. Among those who emigrated, the easy adoption of modern Spanish by Sephardim who went to Latin America, and of Hebrew in Israel, has reduced to near zero the number of people who speak Sephardi Spanish as a first language, while few are able to read it in the Hebrew alphabet in which it was traditionally written.

Sephardi Spanish is often called *Ladino*, though some insist that this term should be restricted to the literal, word-for-word Spanish translation from Hebrew scriptural and liturgical texts which was provided for those who could not read them in the original. Scholars refer to it as *Judeo-Spanish*. The people who speak it call it what it is: *español* (though they would spell the word *espanyol*), and consequently modern Israeli Hebrew calls the language *espanyolit* in contrast with *sefardit* (Spanish of Spain and Latin America).

Though Ladino is dying, there is considerable interest in maintaining the knowledge and use of the language. In particular poetry is published, though in the Latin alphabet which was introduced in the late 1920s when Kemal Atatürk forced it on Turkish. Academic congresses are held, scholarly articles are published and a website forum called *Ladinokomunita* produces large numbers of daily messages in Ladino which are circulated among over a thousand members.

Modern editions of Ladino literature are produced wherever there are interested scholars and willing

---

*from "Sepharad" in the Biblical book of Obadiah, interpreted as meaning Spain

publishers. In Israel the language is protected by the National Authority for Ladino, as well as by academic departments in Israeli universities which teach it and conduct research. In France it is encouraged in the *Institut National pour les Langues et Civilisations Orientales (INALCO)*. Spain's *Consejo Nacional de Investigación Científica* supports research into Ladino. There are research groups in universities in the USA, Switzerland and Germany. Lamentably, Great Britain is backward in this, and only one university has a course in Sephardi studies, though the language itself is not taught.

The aim of this book is to introduce readers to a neglected aspect of Jewish culture which arouses a largely unsatisfied curiosity. For this reason it offers a brief introduction to Ladino literature, and specifically to the novel, with references to further reading. The introduction is given in Spanish as well as in English because the book has been written for speakers of Castilian and Latin American Spanish, as well as for English readers.

The main part of the book is an English translation of *La muz'er onesta*,* a novel by Eliya Rafael Karmona of Constantinople, one of the best-known and most prolific Ladino authors of the late XIX and early XX centuries. The translation is accompanied by a transliteration of the novel from the Hebrew type in which it was printed into the Latin alphabet, following a spelling convention which is intended to reflect the pronunciation of Ladino. Footnotes are provided to clarify the meaning of words which do not exist or are used in different ways in modern Spanish, or of Turkish and French words which entered Ladino from the surrounding world.

---

*On the title page, which uses Hebrew capital or "square" letters, the "zh" sound in muz'er is rendered "z'", but in the text, which uses a slightly different Hebrew type, the sound is rendered as ž. in both cases, the sound is the "s" of the English word "pleasure".

I want to thank my publisher, Ross Bradshaw, of Five Leaves, for his interest and support, the biannual British Judeo-Spanish Studies Conference held at Queen Mary College in London, where Ladino specialists from all over the world meet, its organiser Dr. Hilary Pomeroy, Elena Romero of the CSIC in Madrid, Pilar Romeu of Tirocinio Publishers in Barcelona, Gaëlle Collin of the *Alliance Israélite Internationale* in Paris, Dov Hakohen of the Ben-Zvi Institute in Jerusalem, Leon Yudkin and Helen Beer who helped me formulate ideas about Yiddish. They have all been of great help and encouragement to me. I learned of the existence of Karmona's *La mužer onesta* through Ilana Tahan, Keeper of Hebrew and Jewish material at the British Library, whose inventory of the Ladino holdings of this great library has been of inestimable service to researchers into this endangered manifestation of a great Spanish and Jewish culture.

Michael Alpert
London, November 2008

Introduction

Origins of the Judeo-Spanish Novel[1]

The Jews who arrived in the Ottoman Empire following their expulsion from Spain in 1492 brought the art of printing with them. As well as Hebrew scriptural, liturgical and rabbinic texts, they printed Spanish material in Hebrew characters. This religious and para-religious literature includes translations of the Bible, rabbinic literature, liturgy, and the *Haggadah* or narrative of the Exodus traditionally recounted at the Passover meal. The translations were literal, following Hebrew syntax, and the type of calque language or "translationese" produced is called *Ladino*, although this term is now widely used for Judeo-Spanish or Sephardi (i.e. of Spanish Jews) Spanish in general. From the mid-XIX century onward newspapers, novels, short stories, drama and poetry were also produced in Judeo-Spanish [2].

The most famous of all the religious works in Judeo-Spanish is the *Me'am Lo'ez* ("from a people speaking a foreign language" [Psalm XIV,i]), published in Constantinople in its various parts between 1730 and 1777. This commentary on the Scriptures, accompanied by legal and ethical annotations, was begun by Rabbi Ya'akov Ḥuli[3] (1690-1732), but he finished only his commentary on *Genesis*, while other scholars continued the work. The achievement of the *Me'am Lo'ez* was to offer a continuous and cogent commentary on Scripture in its readers' spoken language. Most of the Spanish-speaking families of the East possessed a volume or at least a few separate parts or pages of this great compendium. From it came the tradition of reading aloud (called *meldar*), usually on a Sabbath afternoon. Such reading became a model for future readers of newspapers and novels[4]. As Rabbi Ḥuli wrote in his introduction:

...Now, when a person comes home from his shop or on the Sabbath or a Festival, when one does not work, he absorbs himself in this book and reads whatever piece he likes[5].

Rabbinic wisdom, which was presented as non-elitist, popular reading, acted as a model, legitimising later translation into Sephardi Spanish of European secular fiction and, ultimately, the creation of original fiction in Ladino itself, the language of the Jews of the Ottoman Empire[6].

Westernisation, Newspapers and Novels

The impulse to write narrative fiction in Sephardi Spanish followed the creation of the Ladino press. Beginning in 1853 with *La Luž de Israel*, there were many titles, mostly short-lived. Among those which lasted longest were *La Buena Esperanza* (1871-1922) and *El Meseret* (1897-1920), published in Smyrna, *La Epoka* (1875-1920) in Salonika, and *El Telegrafo* (1886-1930) and *El Tyempo* (1872-1930), both in Constantinople, as well as the humorous *El Ǧugeton*, edited by Eliya Karmona from 1908 until 1930[7]. Many novels appeared as instalments in these newspapers.

The rise of the Ladino press and novel, with its peak between 1880 and 1930, was contemporaneous with the decadence of the Ottoman Empire and the growth of nationalism in its constituent parts[8]. It also reflected the European Jewish Enlightenment or *Haskalah*. Secular writing in Ladino flourished, however, for little more than fifty years, and ended as the Judeo-Spanish language itself declined, threatened as it was by the cultural hegemony of French from the second half of the XIX century onwards, by the growth of Turkish, Greek and Bulgarian nationalism, by the imposition in Turkey of the Roman alphabet in the 1920s, and finally by the mass murder of the Spanish-speaking Jewish communities of

Greece, Yugoslavia, Rhodes and other territories occupied by the Nazis. Many of the Jewish communities had in any case been weakened and scattered previously by emigration.

The Westernisation of the Eastern Jews began with the arrival, beginning in the 1860s, of the schools of the *Alliance Israélite Universelle*[9]. By 1925, when Eliya Karmona published *La mužer onesta*, Judeo-Spanish readers, imbued with Western values, had been reading secular European fiction for many decades. This was mainly of French origin, in versions translated, adapted or imitated in Sephardi Spanish. In this Jewish readers resembled their neighbours, for the Turkish novel began with translations of Victor Hugo's *Les Misérables* and Daniel Defoe's *Robinson Crusoe*[10]. The mid-XIX century saw the appearance of novels and translations in other languages of the Turkish Empire, while the number of bookshops in Constantinople increased. The context of writing a novel in Judeo-Spanish was like that of other minority languages of the Empire, even Turkish itself, where the word *literature* had always referred to religious texts only. But, as Joseph Nehama observed in his *Histoire des Israélites de Salonique* of 1936:

> On ne commence à se préoccuper de la masse à demi-lettrée que lorsque les écoles ont ouvert une brèche dans les remparts dont s'entoure le fanatisme.[11]

The Judeo-Spanish Novel

Ladino did not enjoy high status among its speakers, for whom the language of prestige was French. Nevertheless, the immense majority of the Jews of Constantinople, Salonika, Smyrna and other cities and towns of the Ottoman Empire used Ladino. It was the language of religious instruction and there was a deep-rooted tradition of publishing Judeo-Spanish religious and para-religious material in Hebrew type, read by both men and women. Despite the attacks launched against Ladino by those who judged it to be no more than jargon, it was the daily means of communication of the Jews of the Balkans and Turkey until the 1930s. Novelists and journalists had to use it to reach their public. There were few secular publications in Hebrew, unlike the large number of periodicals and newspapers read by Jews in Russia and Poland[12]. It is paradoxical that the schools of the *Alliance*, despite their efforts to suppress Ladino, which they called "a bastard jargon incapable of expressing nuances, unsuitable for conveying delicate or elevated ideas..", nevertheless produced those same intellectuals whose writing would use the despised language[13]. The probable reason was that the *Alliance* encouraged intellectual curiosity and thus reading. Strangely, there does not seem to have been much cultural contact between the Spanish-speaking Jews of the East and Spain itself, but nevertheless the period between 1860 and the outbreak of world war in 1914 witnessed an explosion of literary and journalistic creativity in Judeo-Spanish[14].

The major characteristics of the novel in Sephardi Spanish are its dependence on foreign sources and its serialised form of publication. Certainly, a large proportion of Judeo-Spanish fiction was not original, as can be seen by the number of novels whose title pages state that they have been translated, imitated or adapted. Most of the sources are French, including works by Dumas, Hugo, Prévost, Sue, Zola and Jules Verne. One might argue that translation itself is a route to developing one's own style, or on the contrary that the profusion of translation inhibited literary creation in Ladino[15].

The conditions of publication are important. In *La mužer onesta*, a sizeable novella of 111 pages, the general speed of the narration, the shortness of the chapters, the need to write in sixteen-page weekly parts and thus to produce regular moments of drama or significant pause, reflect the conditions faced by harried writers, who often wrote or edited a large part of the newspapers in which their novels were serialised. They wrote against the clock; revision and correction must have been hasty.

Eliya Rafael Karmona

Eliya Karmona was born in Constantinople in 1869 and died there in 1932[16]. He came from an old, respected and well-off family, occupied in civil administration and banking[17].

Karmona attended the infants' school conducted by a teacher or *maestra* and then the standard Jewish elementary school, the *Talmud Torah*, from which at the age of eleven he went to the *Alliance* school. After four years he left, becoming teacher of French to the sons of the Grand Vizir. The Karmona family suffered grave financial losses, however, and Eliya's father ended up as a minor employee in the local tramway system. Eliya lost his job and for some time was reduced to selling matches in the street. Then he was fortunate enough to be taken on as a typesetting apprentice at the newspaper, *El Tyempo*. His wages were insufficient, so he left and spent an adventurous youth in other parts of the Ottoman world including Salonika and Smyrna, travelling as far as Cairo where he suffered real poverty and even hunger. Unsuccessful in his various ventures, he returned to *El Tyempo* where he stayed until 1908.

He had begun to write novels in 1899, when he himself printed *konsežikas* or folktales told him by his mother. Then he began to write novels — his total production totals nearly fifty works[18] — until in 1902 the censor prohibited publications which included robberies, murders and love. Unfortunately, these were the major themes of the Judeo-Spanish novel. Karmona went to Egypt where the censorship was applied less strictly but there were fewer readers of Judeo-Spanish, so, unable to make a living, he returned to Constantinople and *El Tyempo*.

From 1908, when the Young Turks' revolution freed the press and publishers from censorship, Karmona edited and wrote most if not all of his comic weekly, *El Ğugeton*.

In the words of Amelia Barquín, Karmona was,

> ...a sort of Sephardi intellectual frequently found at that time, characterised by his multiplicity of interests and occupations, his energy and participation in many cultural fields, in touch with new values of modernisation...[19]

La Mužer Onesta (The Chaste Wife)

The Ladino novel varies in length but on the whole tends to brevity. To take as examples the novels in the British Library collection[20], most have fewer than fifty pages, and only two or three are sizeable tomes of over two hundred pages. Most of the longer novels are translations, principally from French.

The title page of *La mužer onesta* does not state that it is a translation or an adaptation, though the wife unjustly suspected of infidelity by her husband is a frequent figure in literature[21]. It has 111 pages, of 10 by 14 centimetres, and a total of about sixteen thousand words, which defines it more as a *novelette*[22]. It has 21 chapters (really 19, because it omits numbers six and fourteen, but other chapters are longer). There are seven parts of sixteen pages each. The last page is occupied by an advertisement for the next book (ASK FOR THE NOVEL THE HEARTLESS SISTER-IN-LAW)[23]. It has no publisher in the modern sense. Karmona probably handed his pages directly to the printer, and then passed the printed, cut and bound sheets to Benjamin B. Joseph, a well-known bookseller and distributor. The price is not stated on the page but, but given the poor quality paper and the absence of covers or illustrations, it was probably low enough to be accommodated in the budgets of many families.

Plot of the Novel

The main characters are a young and recently-married couple, Armand and Julietta. He is in business of an unrevealed nature, and although Julietta comes from a poor family, they belong to the prosperous upper middle class. Two servants are mentioned in the novel, and Julietta spends her time visiting her friends. Armand's three friends, Maurice, Richard and Giacomo, do not work either, and are plentifully supplied with money by their wealthy fathers. No more peripheral information is provided. The place where the action takes place is not named and we are not told even that the characters are Jewish. Only the mention of motor cars suggest that the action is contemporary.

One day, soon after his marriage, Armand tells his young wife that he does not like the friendly way she greets their guests. She insists that knowing how to entertain is part of *savoir-vivre* and mere good manners. If he is jealous, says Julietta, he does not really love her. He, reflecting an oriental and *machista* attitude, is proud of his jealousy. Having a history of womanising, he distrusts his wife on principle. Since, in his view, women are weak and cannot resist a persistent seducer, a man who loves his wife should be jealous. Julietta in contrast thinks that women are strong. She claims that a wife who deceives her husband must be unhappy with him. Since this is not her case, she tells Armand that his jealousy is unfounded and will not benefit him. As she says in Chapter Three:

> The more jealous a husband is of his wife the more he obliges her to do something wrong. Fidelity is self-imposed, not forced on a wife by her husband.

Armand, she insists, has no reason to suspect her. She asks him rhetorically, "Have you tested me?" Armand assumes the question is a challenge and decides literally to test her. This is the basis of the plot.

Armand sends his friend Maurice to visit Julietta. Once there, Maurice is to declare his love for her. Although Maurice tries to convince Armand that he has no reason to suspect his wife, and that what he is doing is morally unpleasant, in the end he agrees to do what Armand wants. He visits Julietta, declares his love, and is dismissed forthwith. Julietta insists that she comes from a poor but honourable family and that she will never betray her husband.

When Armand returns home to find out how Julietta has reacted to Maurice's declaration of love, she blames him. His jealousy, she says, has given Maurice a weapon in his attempted seduction. But Julietta soon realises that Maurice was sent on purpose by Armand, who tells Julietta insultingly that she has rejected Maurice only because she suspects it was a trap; yet at the same time Armand denies that he sent Maurice to seduce her. He still, nevertheless, suspects that she is weak and, like all women, easy prey for a determined man. Julietta answers that he is generalising. While she herself will never betray Armand, she claims that a husband's irrational jealousy may well provoke a wife to take a lover.

Maurice, however, now feels genuine passion for Julietta, as will be the case with the other two men whom Armand sends to try to seduce her. The message of the novel is that the danger for a jealous husband is not only that he risks provoking his wife to betray him, but that the seducers may genuinely come to fall in love with the wife, and their false declarations of love may become genuine. Maurice now persuades Armand to let him make another assault on Julietta's virtue, but, in order to improve his seductive technique, he consults Richard, who has the reputation of a womaniser. Richard in his turn is intrigued and decides that he also will try to seduce Julietta. The field is left free for him when she repels Maurice's second attempt.

Richard visits Julietta and is rejected. He, like Maurice, now feels genuine love for her. He confides in another friend, Giacomo, who advises Richard to present Julietta with a pearl necklace. Julietta rejects the gift and dismisses Richard, accusing Armand of having sent him to test her. Armand is actually innocent of this, but he thinks at the same time that it is a good idea. He urges the astonished Richard to try once more to seduce Julietta. Hypocritically pretending embarrassment, Richard is delighted to have Armand's approval.

Discussing their campaign, Richard and Giacomo decide that the latter, an even more skilful seducer, should inveigle himelf into the house of Julietta and Armand in disguise. Once he succeeds, Richard can share Giacomo's triumph. Armand hesitates about bringing yet another man into his scheme, but he is driven by the urge to reassure himself of his wife's fidelity.

Giacomo's plan of action is that Armand should introduce him as an English Lord, who will impress Julietta. But when the "Lord" begins to pay Julietta compliments, she smells a rat, realising that here is yet another man whom her husband has brought to test her fidelity and chastity.

Giacomo, Armand and Julietta go to the theatre. The subject of the play is a jealous husband whose wife leaves him. This allows Giacomo to give some pointed hints to Julietta, who refuses to react. Now Giacomo proposes another plan. During lunch the next day, Armand will find a pretext to depart home hurriedly, leaving Giacomo alone with Julietta. Though beginning to doubt his ability, Giacomo hopes he can manage the seduction.

In the meantime, Julietta confides her worries to her confidante, Madame Clotilde, who advises her that men are all the same. While they talk, an idea suddenly occurs to Julietta. At lunch the next day, she serves chicken. She arranges for herself to have the wishbone (*yades* in Turkish) and invites Armand to play *"Yades"*, a form of forfeits. This game, well-known in the Balkans, requires someone who is given an object, to say *"Yades!"* If the person takes the object without exclaming *"Yades!"* the other has won and the person who accepted the object must pay a forfeit. Armand agrees and they break the bone.

When Armand leaves to go back to his business, as was agreed by him and Giacomo, the latter makes one further effort to seduce Julietta. She pretends some interest and tells him to come to lunch the next day. She explains that, when Giacomo rises to leave the next day, she will accompany him to the door and, in the courtyard, she will hide him in a cupboard. When Armand leaves, she will fetch Giacomo and hints that she may satisfy his desires.

Giacomo thinks he has achieved a victory but he does not tell Armand. As the author explains, "In this way Giacomo deceived his friend." This is the result of Armand's suspicions and his compulsion to test his wife's fidelity.

The next day, Julietta hints to Giacomo that she will surrender to him. When he gets up to leave, she hides him in the cupboard in the courtyard, but she locks it. She comes back to the dining-room and tells Armand that she is very attracted by Giacomo and that the latter is waiting for Armand to leave, at which point Giacomo is expecting to seduce her. Now at last Armand realises that his own behaviour has encouraged Giacomo in his attempted seduction of Julietta and that he has been betrayed by his friend. Armand, furiously threatening to kill Giacomo, demands the key to the cupboard. When Julietta gives it to him and he snatches it she cries *"Yades!"* He has not said *"Yades!"* so he must pay the forfeit, not only by buying her a dress, as previously agreed, but also by abandoning his unjustified suspicions.

Here the novel somewhat suddenly ends. The author repeats the moral and husband and wife live happily ever after.

Commentary

Karmona, an experienced author and newspaper editor, judged the subject of married fidelity and mutual trust to be appropriate and interesting for a novel which he hoped to sell to the Jewish reading public of Constantinople, Salonika and Smyrna of the 1920s, whether or not adultery and the seduction of married women was something that happened as a matter of course among a prosperous and highly westernised section of the Ladino-speaking Jewish bourgeoisie. However, while it may be assumed that the action of the novel takes place in Constantinople in the 1920s and that the characters belong to the Jewish bourgeoisie, this is not actually stated. Moreover, although he had had romantic adventures[24], Karmona, born in 1869, was 56 when he published his novel; he no longer belonged to the generation of its characters. He was describing a world which he did not necessarily know intimately.

Adultery and seduction are, however, frequent themes in the ballads traditionally recited among the Sephardi Spanish speakers of the East. Readers and listeners to *The Chaste Wife* might not have been so shocked at its content as they would have been in a more prudish society[25]. If Constantinople was anything like Salonika as described in 1931 by S. Révah in his novel *Sogeta podrida* (Rotten Society), with its hair-raising accounts of child abuse, prostitution and disease, as well as of extreme poverty and social marginalization, *The Chaste Wife* might be seen as a rather mild alternative for a Sabbath afternoon's reading[26].

In discussing who read this novel, it would be fair to assume that the novel of fantastic "blood and thunder" style adventures, so typical of Ladino narrative fiction, with its bandits, smugglers, thieves and murderers, was less attractive to women readers than a novel of jealousy, an ill-treated wife and attempted seduction such as *The*

Chaste Wife, or *Anna Maria or a Woman's Heart* (1905), written by another Ladino novelist, Alejandro Ben-Ghiyyat, in which the barren and betrayed wife adopts her husband's illegitimate child[27]. The subject of Karmona's novel must have interested its women readers in the same way as in a later generation their daughters and granddaughters would eagerly read gossip magazines about the private lives of film stars, footballers' wives and girlfriends and minor royalty. One can imagine someone reading *The Chaste Wife* aloud, from a newspaper but probably in weekly parts, the form in which it has survived, in the family room, probably on Sabbath afternoons. The women would nudge each other, giving any men who were there meaningful looks every time Maurice, Richard or Giacomo tries to tell Armand how wrong his attitude to Julietta is. How the women must have rejoiced when Julietta, maintaining her dignity, succeeds in showing her husband the consequences of his unreasoning jealousy, consequences that he manages to escape only because of her own chaste behaviour.

Women are often the protagonists in the Judeo-Spanish novel, but Julietta is not the dominating woman, not the seductress, and not the victim of men, but a calm, dignified woman, who achieves her triumph with aplomb and without ridiculing her husband. In her, the *pyedad* or "compassion" that Armand sees as the characteristic of all women does not mean weakness. She is totally the opposite of the idle coffee drinkers and cigarette-smokers, the degenerate oriental Jewish woman described in the reports of the *Alliance* sent to Paris from Turkey[28]. Julietta has adopted Western modes as a result of her education. She does not respond with surprise or embarrassment to the declarations of love made to her by Maurice and the other young men. She protests against their attempts at seduction but not because adultery transgresses the laws of religion or even morality. In this we see her secularization, which does not negate her pride as a faithful wife and her loyalty to her husband.

24

Julietta to some extent reflects the success of an earlier campaign, when in the late XIX century Ladino instructional newspapers such as *El Sol*, *El Amigo de la Familya* and *El Instruktor* saw women as instruments for social progress, while Rosa Gabbay, in her *La cortesiya o reglas del buen comportamyento* (Courtesy or the Rules of Good Behaviour) published in Constantinople in 1871, defended women's education[29].

A Jewish Novel?

There are no Jewish references in Karmona's *The Chaste Wife*, except that the characters speak a Jewish language with occasional hispanicised Hebrew words such as *mazaloso* (lucky), and have Western European first names typical of wealthy Sephardi Jews of the time. However, to adopt the standpoint of David Fresko, the editor of *El Tyempo*, if a Jew reads anything in a language used only by Jews, the text retains its Jewish character[30]. This can be interpreted in the sense of considering how a literary text is *received* by the reader, for only Jews read Karmona's novel.

If *La mužer onesta* is looked at as a Jewish work, inevitably a comparison comes to mind between the literary production of Sephardi Spanish and that of the extensive regions where Yiddish, the mediaeval German which the Jews of the Rhineland had brought with them in the Middle Ages when they moved to Central and Eastern Europe, was the spoken language of most Jews. Superficially, there was some similarity between the positions of Ladino and Yiddish. In both cases the Jews had brought with them a Western European language and had transmitted it down their generations for centuries while they were surrounded by languages quite different from their own. Nevertheless, the comparison may lead to false conclusions. First, the demographics were very different. Yiddish in the late XIX and early XX centuries was the mother-tongue of several million people, whereas it is doubtful if Sephardi Spanish was spoken by more than 300,000. Perhaps for this reason alone, it would be unfair to expect fiction in Ladino to bear comparison with the best of the Yiddish novels of the same epoch.

Another factor to be considered is that, if a novel exists to describe and criticise the society in which it is produced and read, the Judeo-Spanish novel is certainly inferior in comparison with the examination and criticism of Jewish society undertaken by the great Yiddish novelists. Few Ladino novels deal with contemporary society. Even one such as Ben-Yitshak Sacerdote's *Rafael i Miryam*, actually subtitled *Novela de la vida de los ğudiyos de oriente* (A Novel of the Jews of the East), of 1910, hardly corresponds to its subtitle[31]. The absence of Jewish reference in the Ladino novel, particularly to liturgy, Scripture and rabbinic texts, contrasts with the all-pervasive presence of such references and echoes in the contemporary Yiddish novel. Is this because the Ladino novelists had not generally received the intensive Hebrew and rabbinic education of the great Yiddish novelists such as Shalom J. Abramovitz (Mendele Moyker S'forim, 1836-1917), Isaac Leib Peretz (1852-1915) and Shalom Rabinovitz (Sholem Aleykhem, 1859-1916)? The traditional Sephardi educational system had lost prestige to the modern and practical education provided, in the medium of the prestigious French language, in the schools of the *Alliance Israélite Universelle*. The *Alliance* absorbed the *Talmud Torahs* or religious schools. Even so, given the long tradition of studying Bible, particularly *Psalms*, the *Song of Songs*, the Books of *Esther* and *Proverbs*, and the Passover *Haggadah*, verses for the festival of Purim, as well as the *Me'am Lo'ez*, the absence of phraseology or rhythms from such sources seems strange.

The intellectual deterioration of the oriental Sephardi world is reflected also in its comparatively minor creation of theological and jurisprudential material. This may have arisen from the shock administered to the Sephardi world in the XVII century by its perceived error in accepting the claims of the false messiah Shabbetai Zvi and by fears about a resurgence of that or similar movements (the last followers of Shabbetai Zvi, called *Dönmeh*) were still active in Turkey in the heyday of the Ladino novel and to some extent today). The determination of the rabbis to suppress any kind of rational or antinomian tendencies also narrowed intellectual horizons[32]. Finally, the general backwardness of the Islamic world, where there was no Enlightenment as such, was reflected by the tardiness of the Jewish Enlightenment, the *Haskalah*, to flourish in the East.

There may also be linguistic reasons to explain why Sephardi Spanish did not achieve the levels of Yiddish fiction, for while Yiddish was surrounded by European languages, many of which had rich literatures of their own, there was no physical and little cultural connection between Ladino and Castilian Spanish. Thus, when Ladino writers sought new words, or even when they did not really need them, they tended to use the hispanicised French which they learnt in the *Alliance* schools. So, for example, 'to wish' was the French *souhaiter* which became the Ladino *suetar*. In contrast, even in backward Russia, the cultural expectations of Yiddish readers were probably in general more demanding than those of their Ladino counterpart. The great Yiddish novelists, multilingual and very well-read in Jewish and general culture, familiar with the novels of Gogol, Turgenev, Tolstoy and Dostoievsky, enjoyed an audience with no lack of 'ideal' readers. Furthermore, the rich tapestry of Jewish cultural and political life used Yiddish for its purposes, so that the language began to be considered as the appropriate Jewish written language rather than the upper-class Hebrew.

Ladino lacked a narrative tradition. The models for Karmona and the other Sephardi novelists of the East were the great foreign, mostly French, authors, whose

27

wealth of language the Sephardi writers could not imitate. In the Ladino world newspapers and fiction were written in a language which the writers judged suitable for ill-educated people who could not be addressed in the language of greatest prestige, French. Eliya Karmona himself wrote that his motive for using Sephardi Spanish was:

> Having noticed that people who read Spanish are those who cannot read Turkish or French, I began to write in a popular language which even children and old women can understand[33].

Likewise, in 1908, in the first number of his comic newspaper *El Ğugeton*, Karmona wrote,

> *El Ğugeton* is going to be written in a very easy and day-to-day language as we also do in our novels[34]

In this, Karmona was not an innovator. A generation previously, in 1871, Rosa Gabbay, the daughter of Yeḥezkel Gabbay, founder of *El Telegrafo* and a judge in Turkish courts, wrote in the preface to her *La cortesiya y reglas del buen komportamyento* (Constantinople, 1871):

> ...we have made a great effort not to use proper Spanish because this might be difficult for those who do not understand, and we have tried to use oriental Spanish with the hope that this work of ours finds acceptance in the eyes of ladies and gentlemen. It will be for me and for others a great encouragement to continue to translate and publish books to help the progress of our people...

It may then be licit to wonder whether, had the Ladino novel began somewhat earlier and if the French influence on culture had been less, Ladino fiction would have produced its own Mendele or Singer.

How Can Value of the Judeo-Spanish Novel be Judged?

It is hard to apply modern critical methods to the few surviving and accessible copies of the 254 novels that Altabé calculates or the five hundred estimated by Romero[35]. Many novels, published in thin chapbook form without covers, no longer exist physically or are preserved in one copy in a library. Even their presence is difficult to identify because they may be listed under Hebrew because of the type which they use. Only a few have been republished in modern editions[36]. Some of these are listed at the end of this Introduction.

To apply some of the criteria of criticism we may ask whether the Ladino novels are fantasies, or whether they reflect, even obliquely, real life. Did the readers of *The Chaste Wife* identify with or at least recognise Armand, Julietta and the others, their emotions, fears, desires and rancours? Again, do the novels encourage the exercice of moral judgement? Do they challenge the reader's assumptions?

The truth is that we learn little of human relations, real love, jealousy, sacrifice, aspirations or compromise. In general, the Judeo-Spanish novel does not lend itself to sophisticated critical analysis. For one thing, novels which go deeply into the thoughts and emotions of their characters, do so with the help of adjectives and adverbs, elaborate structures of tenses and moods, and a rich vocabulary enabling the author to find the *mot juste* or even to create it. These tools are lacking in the Ladino novel. Its lexis is not rich enough to allow the author to vary his or her choice of words. As a rule, neither the plot nor the characters nor the dialogue are capable of moving a reader who is used to the great European novels.

The Chaste Wife, though it is free of the constraints of place, Jewish relevance, and external events, and can concentrate firmly on its simple plot, lacks internal monologue. Thus there is no development of the deeper thoughts and motives of Armand or Julietta. The author does not use incident to develop the readers' view of the characters. Nor does the omniscient narrator employ indirect discourse to any sustained effect to explain the inner motives of his characters. To be able to do this, an author must have at his disposal a language which can express the minute and varied details of interior and exterior reality. In 1893 *El Tyempo* published a series of articles insisting that Ladino lacked such a wealth of vocabulary to express feelings and ideas[37]. The authors, consequently, had to bring in French words. But would readers of a hispanicised French have understood the thoughts, analyses, generalisations and moral evaluations, the conceptual tools and the modulations of tone, of which French was capable in the hands of a great novelist such as, for example, Flaubert?

The technique of the Ladino novel does not go deeply into individuals' thoughts. In it, people's views are communicated by means of brief conversations in a limited range of vocabulary. In *The Chaste Wife*, expressions are repeated until they become trite and hackneyed, such as *le hižo un calurozo resibo* (she welcomed him warmly) or *Madam, me muero por vos* (Madame, I'm dying for love of you), to the point where the reader can finish the sentence before getting to the end.

The construction of *The Chaste Wife* is sparse. It is a novel with five main characters, who interrelate fictionally for a week or so. There are no long journeys nor long intervals of time. There is only one plot. The novel has the characteristics of a play, with a few loci where the action takes place (Armand and Julietta's house, Armand's office, the street, the hotel where Richard sleeps). Indeed the novel may well have its origin in a play, perhaps by the Armenian Mardoros Minakian, whose work Karmona confesses in his autobiography that he plagiarised[38]. In 1907, in Cairo, Karmona published a novel with a similar subject: *El marido zeloso* (The Jealous Husband), and republished it in 1923[39]. Furthermore, there is some fictional intertextuality in *The Chaste Wife* because the play that Armand, Julietta and Giacomo go to see is on the same subject.

Setting aside the literary merit of the Ladino novel, perhaps it should be considered in the same way as the silent film in the early days of the cinema. The silent film was projected before an unsophisticated audience, who demanded a clear narrative line, with plenty of drama and the raw emotion which could be expressed by the actors' faces and the accompanying music, without reflections and comments by the author or narrator, and which corresponded to and echoed the audience's own preferences and prejudices. Likewise the public which read and listened to the Judeo-Spanish novel being read had seen Ladino printed only in newspapers, in liturgical texts or in the *Me'am Lo'ez*. The novel was a new medium. Furthermore, many of the audience had never read their own language. Few had ever read a novel in another language save at most a few extracts from French classics or the *Fables* of La Fontaine if they had attended an *Alliance* school.

The aim of the Judeo-Spanish novel was to amuse the readers and to sell the newspapers in which the novels were serialised. It does this with its speed and cogency. Yet, although *The Chaste Wife* does not purport to be a novel about the life and morals of a certain class of Jews in Constantinople, it does try to say something about a world which was not too far away from that of at least some of its readers: the Jewish world and the context of marriage, jealousy, infidelity and seduction. The superiority of *The Chaste Wife* arises probably from the very absence of contextual detail, from its concentration on a single subject and from the explicit moral line which it preaches.

To sum up, *The Chaste Wife* is superior to many of the other Ladino novels, but even this work can be classified as a "novelette" with some characteristics of "sub-literature".

Some Contemporary Editions of Judeo-Spanish Novels

Amelia Barquín, "Doce novelas judío-españolas", 1995 (see note 9). L. Carracedo, *El rey i el šastre* (*Estudios Sefardíes,* 1, 1978, 399-410)

M. del Rosario Martínez González, *Historia interesante de el emperador Basil el segundo i el rabi*, under the title *Un marido entre dos mujeres* (Barcelona: Ameller, 1978). There is an English translation by Sita Sheer, *The Rabbi had Two Wives* (Jerusalem, 1985).

Gaëlle Collin, "Edition d'une nouvelle judéo-espagnole. *El ombre de la pendola de Viktor Levi* (Berlin: *Neue Romania*, 22, 1999, 51-70).

Gaëlle Collin. "Eliya Karmona's *La novya aguna* (Berlin: *Neue Romania* 26, 2002)

Pilar Romeu, "Alejandro Perez: *Siempre Ǧudiya* (Granada: *Miscelánea de Estudios Arabes y Hebraicos, Sección de Hebreo*, 46, 1997, 117-135)

Sandra Bennet, "Neglected Heritage of the Jews of the Ottoman Empire from 1885 to 1922" (Thesis, University of London 2004), includes transcriptions of A. Ben-Ghiyyat's *Anna Maria's* and the Ladino adaptation of Bernardin de Saint-Pierre's *Paul et Virginie*.

Footnotes

[1] For a full account of Judeo-Spanish literature *see* Elena Romero, *La creación literaria en lengua sefardí* (Madrid: Mafre, 1992).

[2] *See* Ben-Uri, A., "Ladino in Print. Towards a comprehensive bibliography", *Jewish History* 16 (No.3).

[3] Ḥ represents the Hebrew guttural *ḥet*.

[4] *See* Lehmann, M, "The intended reader of Ladino rabbinic literature and Judeo-Spanish reading culture", in *Jewish History*, 16, No.3, (2002), 283-207.

[5] *Cit.* Romero, 93.

[6] Lehmann, "The intended reader..."

[7] *See* Gaon, M.D.'s list of Judeo-Spanish newspapers, *Ha-Itonut be-Ladino: Bibliografiyya* (Jerusalem: Mossad Ben-Zvi, 1965).

[8] The Treaty of Berlin in 1878 granted independence to Bulgaria, Serbia, Rumania and Montenegro, and the Treaty of London of 1913 left the Ottoman Empire with a tiny rump of territory in Europe.

[9] *See* Rodrigue, A., *French Jews, Turkish Jews; the Alliance Israélite Universelle and the Politics of Jewish Schooling in Turkey 1860-1925* (Bloomington: Indiana University Press, 1990), and Esther Benbassa, "L'Education féminine en Orient; l'école des filles de l'Alliance Israélite Universelle à Galata, Istanbul (1879-1912)", *Histoire, Economie et Société* 4 (1991), 529-559. My grateful thanks to Mlle. Gaëlle Collin for sending me a copy of this article.

[10] Amelia Barquín, *Edición y estudio de doce novelas aljamiadas sefardíes de principios del siglo XX*, doctoral thesis published by Servicio Editorial de la Universidad del País Vasco, Vitoria 1997, 77.

[11] "One begins to concern oneself with the semi-literate masses only when schools have breached the walls with which fanaticism surrounds itself," Quoted in Strauss, J., "Who read what in the Ottoman Empire in the 19th and 20th centuries?" *Middle Eastern Literatures*, 6, 1, January 2003, 39-76. In contrast, see Bennett, S., "Neglected Heritage: the Secular Literature of the Jews of the Ottoman Empire from 1885 to 1922", thesis (2004) read at Queen Mary, University of London, who asks opportunely whether literature would have developed even without the stimulus of the Alliance.

[12] For example, the weekly *Ha-Yom*, of St. Petersburg, printed ten thousand copies. Its successor was *Ha-Tsefirah* of

Warsaw; *Ha-Shiloah* and *Ha-Melitz* appeared in Odessa, while three Hebrew dailies circulated in Warsaw. *See* Sarah A. Stein, *Making Jews Modern: the Yiddish and Ladino Press in the Russian and Ottoman Empires* (Bloomington: Indiana University Press, 2004), 27, 48, 49.

[13] Quotation from an *Alliance* report cited by Henri Nahum, *Juifs de Smyrne XIXe-XXe siècles* (Paris: Aubier, 1977), 102.

[14] *See* Michael Alpert, "Dr.Angel Pulido and Philosephardism in Spain", *Jewish Historical Studies*, 40 (2005), 105-119. *See also* María Antonia Bel Bravo's preliminary study to Pulido's main work *Españoles sin patria y la raza sefardí* (republished Granada, 1993).

[15] María del Rosario Martínez González, *Historia interesante de el emperador Basil el segundo y el rabi*, under the title *Un marido entre dos mujeres* (Barcelona: Ameller, 1978), calculates a total of 303 novels, among which some 130 are original, most of them anonymous, while David Altabé "The Romanso 1900-1933: A Bibliographical Survey", *The Sephardic Scholar*, Series 3, 1977-1978, 96-106 estimates a total of 254 novels of which 115 are original. Elena Romero (*La creación literaria* 221) estimates over five hundred titles.

[16] For Karmona's life the main source is his own partial autobiography, edited as a doctoral thesis by Robyn K. Loewenthal, *Karmona's Autobiography: Judeo-Spanish Popular Press and Novel publishing milieu in Constantinople, Ottoman Empire, Circa 1860-1932*, two volumes, Lincoln, University of Nebraska, 1984. *See also* Marie-Christine Varol, "L'Empire Ottoman à travers la biographie picaresque d'Eliya Karmona", unpublished lecture (my thanks to Mlle. Varol for her kindness in giving me a copy). The autobiography, together with much interesting material from the Ladino press, can be read in Rifat Birmizrahi's compilation *Lo ke meldavan nuestros padres* (Istanbul: Gozlem Gazeticilik Basin Ve Yayin, 2006), published in Judeo-Spanish, Turkish and English.

[17] *See* family tree in Loewenthal, 20.

[18] Loewenthal, 578-609.

[19] Barquín, 87.

[20] *See* Ilana Tahan, "Sephardic and Judeo-Spanish Material in the British Library's Hebrew Collection", *Proceedings of the Thirteenth British Conference on Judeo-Spanish Studies (7-9 September 2003)*, edited by Hilary Pomeroy, (Queen Mary, University of London, 2006), 177-240.

[21] Its plot has some resemblance to Miguel de Cervantes's *El curioso impertinente*. I am grateful to Vicka Prilutsky of the

Hebrew University of Jerusalem for this piece of information, though whether Karmona read Spanish Golden Age literature is uncertain.

22 The small size of each page and the frequency of one-line dialogue explain why each page contains only approximately 150 words.

23 *Sic,* all in square Hebrew capitals.

24 *See* Varol, typewritten text *cit.* Karmona married Rachel Levi, who was head of the girls' school of the *Alliance* at Ortoköy. Gabriel Arié, head of the boys' school, liked her, but found her ways "a bit too free". *See* Gabriel Arié, *A Sephardi Life in South-Eastern Europe. The Autobiography and Journal of Gabriel Arié 1863-1936,* edited by Esther Benbassa and Aron Rodrigue (Seattle: Washington University Press, 1998), 76.

25 On morality among Jewish women in the epoch *see* Benbassa, "L'éducation féminine..." *cit.*

26 Suzy Gross, of Bar-Ilan University, Tel-Aviv, presented a description of *Soğeta podrida* at the Fifteenth Conference of Judeo-Spanish Studies, held at Queen Mary, University of London on 29-31 July, 2008 (in press).

27 Readers of the Spanish novel will recognise this as the plot of Benito Pérez Galdós's *Fortunata y Jacinta* (Madrid, 1887), but there is no evidence that Ben-Ghiyyat read it.

28 Some are quoted in Rodrigue, *French Jews,* 78.

29 For *El Instruktor see* Stein, 127.

30 Stein, 125.

31 See David Altabé's summary in "Parallels in the Development of Modern Turkish and Judeo-Spanish Literature", *Studies on Turkish-Jewish History* (New York: Sepher-Hermon Press, 1996), 56-72.

32 This is suggested by Ya'akov Barnai in Goldberg, H (ed.), *Sephardi and Middle East Jewries: History and Culture in the Modern Eras (Bloomington: Indiana University Press, 1996),* 73-80, especially pages 75 and 79. *See also* Esther Benbassa and Rodrigue, A., *Sephardi Jewry: a History of the Judeo-Spanish Community 14th-20th Centuries* (Berkeley: University of California Press, 2000), 60.

33 "Avyendo remarkado ke el ke melda el espanyol, es akel ke no conose ni el turko ni el franses, yo empesi a eskrivir en un linguaže popular ke mismo kriaturas i vyežas lo entendiyan". Cit. Birmizrahi, 508.

34 "*El Ğugeton* va a ser eskrito en un linguaže mui fasil i mui koryente sigun azemos tambiyen por nuestros romansos".

35 Romero, 221.

35

[36] For this reason alone, Ilana Tahan's inventory of the British Library's Ladino holdings is so valuable.

[37] Stein, 73.

[38] Loewenthal, 45.

[39] Loewenthal, 588 and 601.

The Chaste Wife

by Eliya R. Karmona
First published Constantinople 5685
(1924-1925)

*Translated with an introduction
by Michael Alpert*

Chapter 1

It was a Monday morning. Armand Fredol and Julietta Gaskarin, who had been married for only two weeks, were sitting facing each other exchanging the sweet nothings of their honeymoon. Julietta was happy and laughed with her husband as she said:

"Thank God, after three years of sincere love, God was so good as to unite our hearts."

Armand smiled at these words as he looked at her with one of those glances which makes the heart beat faster, and he listened to his new wife continue in the same vein:

"Please tell me, Armand, was it my beauty that you fell in love with?"

"Of course. If you weren't beautiful I would never have married you."

"But what about my personality? Don't I have an attractive personality?"

"Yes, darling, very much so. I must congratulate myself on choosing a wife with such a delightful personality."

"And my education?"

"That leaves nothing to be desired either. Only — don't be annoyed, Julietta — I'm going to tell you something."

"Go on, Armand darling. Is there something wrong with me? I'll do something about it at once."

"No, darling, there's nothing wrong... but there's something that makes me feel strange whenever I see it in you."

"Armand! Please explain what you mean. I want to know what I'm doing wrong and correct it. What is it that you don't like in me?"

"There's nothing I don't like, darling, but I often notice that when some guest comes you're very friendly with him. And I don't like it, that's the truth."

"But that's just good manners."

"Yes, if you didn't clasp his hand and smile at him,

wouldn't you say?"

"Simple courtesy means we have to welcome all our visitors warmly, whether it's a woman or a man. I don't think you can attach any special meaning to my shaking his hand."

"But, darling, it upsets me. I'm jealous. I feel embarrassed."

"You're jealous? If you're jealous, it shows that you don't really love me."

"Just the opposite, darling Julietta, when a husband loves his wife he must be jealous."

"Nonsense! A man should not be jealous of his wife, nor she of him. It's nonsense. If both are sincerely in love then neither could possibly betray the other."

"Yes, of course you're right, darling, but there's one important point here that not many people understand."

"Married only a fortnight and getting jealous already! You should be ashamed!"

"Don't be cross, darling. Women aren't bad, but they are tender-hearted and when a man who comes visiting sees that you're being nice to him, he takes advantage of your kindness to tell you that he loves you, says that he is dying for love of you, weeps for hours at your feet, and you women, with your tender hearts, feel sorry for him and give him what he wants."

"I think you are forgetting that we women are born clever. A wife never betrays her husband if she is happy with him. If you see women who trick their husbands there is a purpose in it. Either she doesn't like him, or he's been unfaithful to her, or the life that the husband gives his wife doesn't fit her idea of how to live. But I'm sure that you and I love each other sincerely, that you are a model husband, as I know you are, and that we have the same level of education. And if as a husband you leave nothing to be desired, why should your wife deceive you? No, Armand, don't be jealous, because jealousy will make you suffer. No man should be jealous of his wife, nor any wife of her husband. It's silly. There's no reason, no cause for it, and you get no benefit and only worry every day."

"Maybe so, but what can I do? I *am* jealous! And I'm jealous just because I love you so very much!"

Julietta smiled at the reply. She took her husband's hand, put it over her eyes and said to him:

"Don't be jealous, Armand, don't be jealous. You've had the *mazal** to find a chaste woman."

"I know. I don't suspect you, but it's just my nature. I can't help it."

"So, there's no need to bring any visitors to the house and we don't have to go anywhere. We have to live a solitary life, do we?" replied Julietta with some anger in her voice.

Armand realised that his wife was cross, so he changed his tone, hugged and kissed her gently and said:

"Don't be cross, darling, I shan't be jealous. Happy now?"

"Of course. What is jealousy? It's shameful. Being jealous means that you don't trust your wife. And a husband should never distrust his wife if he doesn't test her. Have you tested me and found me unfaithful?"

This answer made young Armand shiver with pleasure. His wife had told him to test her! This was a good way of checking if she was deceiving him.

They talked about other things for another half hour. Armand dressed, said goodbye to Julietta and went off to business.

**mazal* (Hebrew): luck

Chapter 2

When Armand went out he no longer felt as happy as he had done at home half an hour earlier. The remarks that his wife had made about jealousy had hurt him. And the word "test" that Julietta had used, gave him cause to think. He really loved his wife, and consequently it wasn't a bad thing to be jealous, but seeing that this merely angered his wife he felt he had to do what she said by giving in to his wish to test her to see if she was chaste and if the friendly reception she gave their male guests was merely a matter of good manners or whether it was to attract the interest of one of them.

Now he had to think. How could he test his wife? Who could he tell in confidence that he wanted to test Julietta? Could he really play this rather scandalous game?

He worried and worried about this, and when he arrived at his business he was sad and preoccupied. His head clerk was puzzled.

"What's the matter, Sinyor Armand? Why are you so sad?"

"Nothing's the matter," replied Armand. "Please go and fetch Sinyor Maurice Fluss, my partner's son. I need to talk to him about an important matter."

Five minutes later, Maurice was there.

"Oh, you're here already! Good!" exclaimed Armand. "Let's go out, I've got something important to talk to you about."

Taking Maurice by the arm, Armand left the store and went and sat in a bar. He ordered two beers.

"Drinking beer so early?" asked Maurice.

"It doesn't matter. I have to tell you a secret that's for your ears only."

"I must say, Armand, you're worrying me."

"There's no need for you to worry. I only want some advice."

"You want *me* to advise you? You're older than me."

"I know, but sometimes younger people know more than older ones."

"Tell me then. What's the matter?"

"You know that you are I are two close friends. We've been together since we left school and we've shared many secrets."

"That's true enough."

"You also know that for many years I played about and had women like one has a glass of lemonade."

"That's true also."

"Well, since I know just how easy women are, I'm worrying about my wife. She's very slim, charming, she knows how to behave and she gives a warm welcome to every visitor we have."

"She's only doing what she ought to."

"Yes, that's true but... I don't like it. You know that in this world it's not a good idea to be warm and friendly to every man who comes visiting. It gives him the wrong idea and, one day... who knows?... Oh, I don't know how to say it."

"You're right, of course. Even a thief should always be suspicious that someone might be going to rob *him*. But do you think that all men are like you? When you used to meet a woman, a minute later you were trying to get her into bed. But all women aren't the same. You should know this because you were courting for three years and you yourself told me that you had met a chaste woman for the first time."

"Yes, that's true... I don't know what to say."

"You've only been married for two weeks. Are you jealous already?"

"Yes, I am. This morning while we were having coffee, Julietta and I talked about my jealousy. She was very upset when I told her I was jealous. The only answer she gave was: You can't be jealous if you don't test me."

"You want to test her?"

"Exactly."

"You're mad."

"Mad? Why?"

"It's obvious. If you put a match next to a fire to see if it bursts into flame of course it will."

"That's not the same thing. A woman doesn't fall in love with a young man like a match catches fire."

"Do what you like, I think you're wrong."

" Maybe you don't think like me. I only want to ask you to do me a favour."

"About this?"

"Yes."

"What can I do?"

"I want you to try to test my wife."

"I... test her? How?"

"By telling her you love her."

"What! You want me, your partner's son, to tell your wife that I love her?"

"Precisely, that's exactly it. If my wife is used to love affairs, she'll accept your proposition at once, but if she is chaste, as soon as you make your move, she'll throw you out and tell me all about it."

"You know, I really don't want to get into anything of this sort."

"What harm will it do? Now, you're going to go to my house straightaway with the excuse that you've come to tell my wife not to expect me because I'm going to have lunch with a friend. Profiting from my absence, you're going to stay there for a bit, start talking to her and then say that you are in love with her. If she accepts, we'll both know the truth. If not, ask her not to say anything, and if she keeps your secret and doesn't tell me about it, it means that she keeps secrets from me and that you've still got a chance with her. Then I'll send you a second and a third time, and that's how I'll test my wife's faithfulness."

"You must be very happy at home but now you want to change all that joy into sadness."

"I must be sure of what I have."

Maurice thought for a while and then he said:

"I'll go just as a favour to you, but this is not a good idea."

"You go, the rest is up to me."

Young Maurice put his hat on and went to pay a visit to the house which we already know.

Chapter 3

From the moment that Armand left home after the conversation that our readers have learned about, Julietta was sad and depressed. Involuntarily, a stab in her heart made her cry.

"Woe is me!" she exclaimed, "Why did I, daughter of a poor man, marry this rich husband? Plenty of money, but what sort of life? We've been married for only two weeks and he's jealous already. God knows if soon he won't forbid me even to go out. Jealous!...What's jealousy? If I'm a bad woman, fifty jealousies aren't worth a copper coin, because the more a man suspects his wife, the more he forces her to be a bad woman. Chastity comes by itself, not from one's husband's orders!"

She was saying that, when suddenly the manservant came to tell her that Sinyor Maurice Fluss, the son of her husband's partner, had arrived and was asking to see her.

"Show him into the drawing-room," she said.

And Julietta walked into the drawing-room, and stood awaiting her visitor.

When Maurice entered the room Julietta went to receive him, as she said:

"Welcome, Sinyor Maurice, I'm surprised to see you during the day and on a weekday too."

"No need to worry, Madame. Since your husband heard that I had to come this way, he asked me to tell you that he's not coming home for lunch because he's been invited elsewhere."

"Thank you, Sinyor Maurice, and I hope you will excuse the inconvenience that this errand for my husband may have caused."

"Oh, not at all, Madame, on the contrary, this errand has been very welcome, because to tell you the truth, I wanted very much to see you, and coming here suits me perfectly."

46

"You wanted to see me?" exclaimed Julietta. "That's strange. You are here most nights, so why do you want to see me now?"

"That's true, but... Madame, you don't know... Just now, talking to your husband, I told him he was the luckiest man in the world, having a wife like you, and I told him that he doesn't appreciate you as I do."

"And didn't my husband react to this? Didn't his colour change?"

"A little."

"He is very jealous, but he doesn't know that his wife is chaste."

"All wives are chaste, but... Madame... sometimes something grows in the garden that the gardener doesn't want. Sometimes, without being able to stop herself, a woman can fall in love with a man just like that, without actually wanting to, I have fallen in love with you, and that's what I meant just now when I said I wanted to see you."

"These words made Madame Julietta change colour, and she replied very calmly:

"You are knocking at a firmly-closed door, Sinyor Maurice, I am not one of those aristocratic women who appeal to the hearts of men for their own pleasure and their luxuries. No, Sinyor, I'm the daughter of a poor man, whose only capital was uprightness, and that's the way I was brought up."

"But Madame, have a little pity. I've always found women very merciful."

"Yes, we are, but for giving charity to people who need pity."

"So, Madame, am I not going to have the good fortune to receive a favourable response from you?"

"Never! Although my husband is jealous and a jealous man deserves to be deceived, I'll never betray him."

"But, Madame, I'm dying for you. Life is very bitter without you."

"So pour a little sugar in it and make it sweeter. I can

47

never betray my husband!"

"So, must I abandon all hope?"

"Certainly, Sinyor Maurice, try knocking on another door."

Maurice stood up to take his leave, but Julietta did not give him her hand as she said:

"Goodbye, Sinyor Maurice, don't upset yourself, don't be embittered. There are many women around who can certainly sweeten your life for you."

Maurice departed and Julietta, now alone, said to herself:

"Only a little earlier I was talking to my husband about jealousy, and half an hour later this gentleman, who claims to be my husband's friend, tells me he loves me. It's a strange sort of love, if somebody else has to suggest it."

She thought for a while, and then exclaimed:

"I've got it! That devil's trying to trick me. It's nobody else! This morning, while we were talking, I told my husband to test me before suspecting me. He must have sent Maurice to test me! That's it. It can't be anything else! So much the better. Maurice's answer will show him again that I am a faithful wife. What an imbecile of a husband! He knows that if a woman wants to do something bad, neither tests nor suspicions make any difference. She knows how to pick her moment without him knowing. What an idiot! He just doesn't appreciate what he has in me."

Chapter 4

Our jealous Armand was impatiently awaiting Maurice's arrival."

"Chaste women are very rare," he was saying to himself, "and I'm sure Maurice will have his way with her."

For two and a half hours he walked up and down his office, lighting and stubbing out cigarettes.

Suddenly his eyes lit up. Maurice had just come into the room.

"It's you, Maurice! Did it go like I said?"

"God made her very tough, you're very lucky to have a faithful wife."

"You've discovered that so soon?"

"Bah! You don't need much time to find out. The things I said to her and how I begged her would have melted a heart of stone."

"Maybe she behaved like that the first time. If you go on visiting my house regularly she may give in."

"But she threw me out, *mon cher*, because I was bold enough to clutch her hand."

"So you think my wife is chaste?"

"Of course. She's more than chaste."

"One proof doesn't convince me. I must have another. Tomorrow I'll find someone else to test her."

"You're obviously stupid, and really an idiot! Your wife will see that I went there today and someone else is going tomorrow, so she'll remember very soon that she told you to test her, and she'll realise that that's just what you are doing."

"So what should I do?"

"Wait a month at least, and then send somebody else."

"That's a good idea. You're right. All the same, I'll wait a week."

"Only, there's something you should think about, and you're not thinking about it, before you send an inspector to examine your wife's heart."

"And what's that?"

"You yourself can test whether your wife is faithful, and you don't need anybody else."

"How can I test her?"

"It's obvious that your jealousy is clouding your brain."

"I don't know what you mean."

"I mean that when you go home tonight, if your wife doesn't tell you anything about what happened today, it means that she is happy with my proposition and that maybe there's some chance. But if she receives you with an angry face, tells you the story and says nasty things about me, it means that her refusal was serious and that she is faithful."

"That's a good idea! I'm not going to wait till tonight. I'm going straightaway and if she asks me why I've come home so early, I'll say that I missed her and that I came home to take her out. Bravo, Maurice! You've thought it out well. I'm off at once."

Without letting Maurice say one word more, he put on his hat and went home.

Chapter 5

Madame Julietta was now sure of what she had thought, but she wanted to be absolutely certain of her suspicions. So she was thinking how she could discover her husband's intentions when the door opened suddenly and Armand, with a smile on his face, came into the room.

"You're worrying me!" exclaimed Julietta, "what are you doing at home at this time of day?"

"I think you're forgetting, darling, that we're on our honeymoon. I missed you and I've come to see you."

"It's a pity you didn't come a little earlier. You would have seen a fine pantomime."

"Why? What happened? Was there a fire?"

"No, no fire, but a man came to see if he could put his own fire out."

"Put his own fire out? A man came here?"

"Yes, one of your very sincere friends, whom you think of like a brother."

"Who's that?"

"Your friend Maurice."

"What was Maurice doing here in the daytime?"

"How should I know? He came to visit and I received him in the usual way, but the wretch had hardly sat down than he said he was in love with me, that he was dying for me, and lots of other things that quite took me aback."

"And what did you say?"

"I sent him packing."

Armand pretended to be considering this as Julietta went on:

"So you can see what some friends are like, I mean those people you think are genuine friends of yours. But it's not them who should be blamed. It's your fault."

"My fault? What have I done?"

"Of course it's your fault. You tell all your friends that you are jealous, and a jealous husband angers his wife so much that in the end she does deceive him, and that's the first thing he said as he tried to seduce me. He came in and the very first thing he said was:

'I'm very sorry for you, Madame Julietta, because you're a beautiful woman, lovely, charming, and to have a jealous husband must be very unpleasant. If you would only love me you would have a very pleasant life.'

And as he said that, he talked about the wonderful life I would have with him and the awful time I was going to have living with a jealous husband."

"And what did you say to him?"

"What do you think I said? I told him he was knocking on the wrong door and that he should look somewhere else. I've been married for only two weeks, but if it was two weeks or even 150 years, I would never try to deceive my husband."

Armand began to laugh, and Julietta, trying to make him tell her what she wanted to know, came close to her husband, talked to him persuasively and with her arms around him, said:

"Now Armand, if I ask you something will you tell me what I want to know?"

"Of course."

"But what if it's something you don't want to tell me."

"Between a husband and wife who love each other there can't be any secrets, I know. You should know that as well, and what you know I should know. I mean if your love is as sincere as mine."

"That's it! I suspected you! The way Maurice was talking and the pitiful looks he was giving me, his little laughs, all that made me think that you had sent him to test me."

"And is that why you didn't give him what he wanted?"

"Take that back, Armand! You said you loved me, and if you love me you should tell me if what I thought is true. I'm telling you now and I'll always tell you. You can test me not only with Maurice but with twenty others like Maurice! I'll never think of betraying my husband!"

"Look, Julietta. I didn't tell Maurice to come. The wretch tried to trap you because you're so beautiful. Now to assure you of what I am saying, let me say that I no longer suspect your chastity. Our love is new, and even if I were the worst of husbands, it's still early for you to betray me with another. All the same, I told you, and I'll tell you again and again that women are not bad, but you are very soft-hearted. Some men are real devils and they know how to steal hearts with their false promises and oaths. Even the most stubborn woman's heart can soften."

"Is that what people have told you, and do you think it is true?"

"My experience of life makes me believe it."

"You're completely mistaken! All women are not the same, any more than all men are alike. I'm telling you now and I'll keep telling you. I'm faithful and I beg you not to suspect me, because it's jealousy that turns a woman towards infidelity."

"You're wrong in that."

"No, I'm right. Still, let's stop arguing! Now that you've come back home during the morning, do you want to have lunch here?"

"Yes, that's why I came."

"Really?" exclaimed the woman with a smile, and calling the maid, she told her to get lunch ready.

Chapter 7
(*sic*, as numbered in the original publication)

A man can trust another with everything he has, gold, silver, jewels, houses etc, but when it comes to making him his wife's guardian and inspector of how she behaves, every husband should think deeply first, and be very, very careful whom he chooses for this mission. We learn this precisely from this story, as our readers are going to see.

When Maurice left Julietta's house, having carried out the task that Armand had entrusted to him, he didn't leave as he had entered. He had something more in his heart! And this was the love he felt for Julietta. He had often come and gone from Armand's house, and Julietta had seemed just another woman. But this time, face to face with Julietta, and talking a great deal about deep matters, Maurice found Julietta to be a woman who touched his heart. He had gone to try to seduce her, but his heart told him to take her and a voice from his heart said to him:

"This is the woman you want. This is the women you need!"

This is why he was impatiently waiting for Armand to come back to his office.

"If this woman keeps quiet about my declaration of love, it means that she is willing and that, as with all women, I'll have to be more persistent. But if she tells her husband everything I said to her, then I'll find it very hard to succeed with her. In any case, I must have her at all costs. She has inflamed my heart! Wait till Armand comes, I'll have to decide from what he says what I must do."

And our young Maurice, burning with love for Julietta, began to wait impatiently for Armand to arrive. But as we have seen, the latter had stayed at home for lunch, so far two and a half hours our young Maurice waited impatiently without a bite to eat, lighting and stubbing out cigarette after cigarette.

It was just after three o'clock when the door suddenly opened and Armand came in with a smile on his face.

"What news? Did things turn out like I said they would?"

"Exactly. After she told me everything you had said, she realised also that I sent you and that you were there to test her."

"And did you admit it?"

"Not at all, I pretended I knew nothing about it and went as far as calling you a coward in front of my wife."

"That was the right thing to do, because if you had admitted your trick, I couldn't go to your house again."

"Right, that's over. What are we going to do now?"

"What do you want to do?"

"Test my wife. I must know if she is faithful, whatever it takes."

Maurice thought and a few moments later he replied:

"Now that your wife knows that I didn't go to test her on your behalf, do you want me to go back and try to seduce her?"

"You'll get the same reply as the first time."

"That's true, but you don't know how women behave. Even the most immoral one won't give you what you ask the first time. Only by talking to her, by begging, can you soften a woman's heart."

"You think you're right in what you're saying?"

"Surely."

"But I thought it would be better to send somebody else."

"Not at all, because if the second one fails you'll send a third, and if the third doesn't succeed you'll send a fourth and one day you'll make an arrangement with a friend who has a loose tongue and he'll tell your wife what you're doing. But when it's just one man who keeps going, then every time he goes he can say something else, and so he has a chance of knowing what she really feels in her heart."

"You're right, I agree with your way of thinking, so come and go as you like. All I want you to do is to test whether my wife is faithful or not."

Chapter 8

You can imagine how happy Maurice was when he received Armand's permission to visit Julietta every day.

"Going in and out of Julietta's house every day I'm sure to succeed! Of course, at the beginning, a woman doesn't give in easily, but if I persist I'm sure to win in the end."

He left Armand, promising that he would go and visit his wife the next day. Out he rushed into the street like a madman to think out a way to carry out his plan.

After thinking through many plans and ideas, he remembered his friend Richard.

"This friend can be very useful to me. Richard knows how to snap up ten women in as many minutes. I'll go to him and take a few lessons this morning."

Having taken this decision, Maurice went straight to Richard to tell him what we already know about the story so far.

Young Richard was the son of a rich banker. He knew how to spend money without worrying because his father, as well as being very rich, worked every day and all his profits went to his spoiled son, who went to the bank for only two or three hours a day.

The day Maurice decided to go and see Richard, the latter was very deep in thought. He felt he had had enough of all his vices, that his actresses were costing him huge sums of money, and he wasn't the only one to whom they gave their favours. He had decided to settle down, but not with a wife, because he was sure he would tire of her also. He had decided to take a mistress who would be faithful to him alone.

He was thinking about this, when he saw his friend Maurice approach and greet him:

"Good day, Richard."

"Good day, Maurice."

"I've come to ask you a favour, or rather some advice."

"What's it about? Is it a woman?"

"Exactly."

"Tell me. I see you suffer from the same illness as me."

"With one small difference. You can have what you want, but I can't."

"You can get everything with money."

"Not everything, my friend. I would give all I my capital to have the woman I love."

"Is she beautiful?"

"Very beautiful! But... very chaste, very faithful to her husband."

"What do you want me to advise you?"

"What to do so as to have her."

"Ask her every day, tell her you are dying with love for her, beg her, implore her, until her heart softens and she gives in. Can you tell me who this woman is?"

"The wife of our friend Armand."

"What! The one who got married two weeks ago?"

"Precisely."

"She's a beautiful woman. You're right. You must do what I told you."

"But you don't know the obstacles."

"What obstacles?"

In a few short words, Maurice told Richard what our readers already know about Julietta's categorical refusal.

His account made Richard think, and he said to himself:

"Here's a good answer to what I need. I know what I can do. I'm sure to succeed."

Looking up, he said to Maurice: "Will you introduce me to this lady?"

"What for?"

"To teach you how to deceive a woman."

"And you'll take her away from me."

"I shan't do that, but I might ask you for part of the profit."

"Let me try once or twice more, and then, if I don't succeed, I'll ask for your help."

"Agreed."

Maurice said goodbye to his friend, went out and straight to the scene of his previous defeat. As he arrived at the door, he stopped, thinking:

"Ah! I'm not going twice in the same day. I'll leave it for tomorrow."

He spent that night doing this and that, waiting impatiently for day to come. And when he calculated that Armand had left home, he went to visit Madame Julietta. She received him in a slightly less friendly way than usual, and pointed to a chair.

Maurice sat down and began to speak.

"Excuse me, Madame, for bothering you once more. My late father said that time is the great remedy for all things. Everything comes with time. In these last twenty-four hours have you not been thinking a little about this slave here in front of you, dying for your love?"

"I never thought about you, you didn't even come into my mind."

"Nevertheless, Madame, you should have some pity for me. I'm going mad for you and a refusal from you would put my life in danger."

Julietta smiled mockingly as she replied:

"That approach leaves me cold. I've heard it from many men. Neither Sinyor Maurice, nor many other men like Sinyor Maurice, can destroy my honour, and that's precisely why I want to ask you to do something for me as a favour."

"Command me, Madame, your slave is ready to obey all your orders."

"I've no command to give you. What I have to say to you is that if you're going to come here to my house you must come honourably as you used to. But if you have the idea, every time that you come, of destroying my husband's honour and mine, kindly don't come again."

"Are you throwing me out of your house, Madame?"

"I'm not throwing you out, but you are asking to be thrown out. I've already told you there is nothing you can get from me. I am a married woman, living a loving life with my husband, and I've never thought of selling my honour. It's up to you to decide what you want to do."

"But, Madame Julietta, you don't believe what I say. I love you! I adore you! Please have some pity on me!"

"Before I pity you I must have some for myself."

"So? Must I hope for even longer?"

"Hope? Give up hope, rather."

"But Madame, you are taking vengeance on me!"

"Get me out of your mind, Sinyor Maurice. I can give you nothing. Knock on some other door."

And Julietta stood up and without a word to Maurice, she left.

Chapter 9

For the moment let us leave Maurice suffering in vain, while we see what young Richard is going to do after his talk with Maurice. As we said, he was fed up with running after women and he wanted to settle down with just one.

What Maurice said made him remember the beauty of Armand's wife. He had seen her only once and had admired her without being able to do anything about it, given that she was his friend's wife. But when Maurice came to ask his advice he forgot about what was right and proper and began to think about what he wanted.

At first he thought of sending her a letter, filling it with those words that send a shiver down a woman's back. But he soon changed his mind and decided to pay a visit to that lady. He had seen her only once, on the day of her marriage.

He made up his mind at once and that same afternoon, before Maurice went there, he rushed to Armand's house.

The maid opened the door, he showed his visiting card and five minutes later, Richard was in Madame Julietta's drawing room. She welcomed him very elegantly and asked him to sit in a luxurious armchair.

"Madame, please excuse the importunate nature of my visit," said Richard, "I met you only on your wedding day, but I have something to tell you which makes it essential to come and see you."

"What is it about, Sinyor?"

"I came to tell you that the life of a young man of 28 is in danger, and that only you have the medicine that can save him."

"You would do well to explain yourself rather more clearly. I don't understand you."

"But, Madame, I don't know how I have the courage to speak to you! From the moment I first set eyes on you, on your wedding day, I fell head over heels in love with you. For two weeks I haven't been able to eat or sleep. I held back, because I didn't want to betray my friend Armand. But I can be patient no longer, and I have come to throw myself at your feet and beg you to have pity on me, or you will condemn me to despair and suicide."

And Richard pretended to be about to weep.

Julietta observed her guest closely, and said to herself: "Here's another pest coming to drive me mad!"

Sitting up very straight, she smiled mockingly and replied:

"How the world has changed! Friends have become false. You just said that my husband is your friend, so how can you dare to dishonour someone you call a friend?"

"You are right, Madame, I know that what I am doing is a crime, but what can I do? I've lost my heart to you. I've tried over and over again to forget, but I can't. It's despair which has forced me to come and beat at the door of your merciful heart."

"You're certainly knocking on the wrong door! My heart is not soft. It's very hard. I needed someone to whom to entrust my heart. I found him, I gave him my heart and now nobody except my husband can win it again."

"Do you want a young man to die because of you?"

"Nobody dies for a woman, if he has any sense at all. I can't speak for a madman."

"But Madame, you forget that Cupid's arrows can kill someone."

"That's for those who allow themselves to be wounded, but people who have good judgement understand quite well that they shouldn't keep on hoping for something which they can't ever have."

"I swear, Madame, that I didn't think you had such little pity."

"I have pity for the poor and the sick... but when people want to stain my honour, I have pity for myself first before anyone else."

"But Madame, believe me, I'm desperate."

"I don't care. If you are mad go to the hospital. I understand that you have fallen for me and to try and slake your desire you've come to tell me you love me. That was a good idea if you might have got somewhere, but now that you know that there's nothing to gain, you should give up the idea."

"But I cannot."

"Yes you can, Sinyor Richard. You came here because you are madly in love with me and you don't want to die of love. So now tell yourself that there's no chance, Tell yourself 'I don't want to die' and you won't die. I don't think I'm the only woman in the world. There are many other women better than me. Tell one of them you love her and you'll see that I'm right. You'll feel the same love for her that you do now for me."

This reply did not convince Richard. He tried to go on talking, but Julietta stopped him and said: "Don't wear yourself out in vain, Sinyor Richard. It's true that I had some adventures before my marriage, but now my heart belongs entirely to Armand and nobody else can have it. So let me tell you once more. You can come here as a friend, but never with bad intentions because you won't be successful. I won't throw you out today, but if you ever come again and say you love me, I tell you now that I'll show you the door."

At this, Richard could think of nothing else to say and got up to say goodbye. As he moved to take Julietta's hand, she said: "There's no need, Sinyor Richard. It's like eating some salad to give you an appetite when you've had the meal already. Now you know there's nothing for you, letting you touch my hand would do you more harm than good."

And poor Richard left, sad and downhearted, having failed, for the first time, to deceive a woman.

Once alone, Julietta began to laugh like a child as she exclaimed: "It's a strange world. When I was a girl and wanted to get married, nobody came to declare his love

for me. Now I'm wed, they all come sniffing round me...
pointlessly. They won't get anywhere. The duty of a married woman is to be chaste. If she isn't, the children she bears are corrupted. Besides, love between husband and wife is sincere only when neither loves another. If one of them does love somebody else, woe to him, there will be a third and then a fourth. If the men don't come, the woman herself looks for them.

No! No! I must not give my heart to anybody! I must live and die faithful!"

Chapter 10

When Richard left Julietta he did not know what to do. When he had gone there it was simply to see if he could seduce a woman. But scarcely had he found himself in Julietta's presence and started to talk, the sweet and gentle way she spoke sent a shaft through his heart, and every time that Armand's wife refused his ardour, his heart burned with love and by the time he left he was madly in love with the beautiful Julietta.

With this and the challenge of her refusing him, he wanted to have her at all costs, even spending madly on whatever it took, but how could he succeed now that Julietta had told him that she could not sell her heart to another man?

He was walking along the street like a madman, pre-occupied, with his head down, taking no notice at all of people who were nodding to him. He was walking with his eyes on the ground when suddenly he bumped into a man and looked up to excuse himself.

"Are you really so busy, Richard?" asked Giacomo, a friend of Richard's who had knocked his arm.

"Oh, friend, don't ask. I've got something on my mind and I can't even think straight."

"What's the problem?"

"Oh. Giacomo! You don't know the sort of life I lead. For nearly ten years I've been indulging in vices, but I've never fallen in love with a girl. Unfortunately, I've recently got mixed up with a woman and I'm dying with love for her."

"Dying with love? But you've got a good position and you can quite easily marry her."

"Unfortunately not. She's married."

"Married!"

"Yes, and to a friend of mine."

"So, how can you dare fall in love with her?"

"How can I dare? Don't you know that once you're in love there are no boundaries. I saw her, I liked her, I fell in love with her."

"And have you told her you love her?"

"Yes, I have."

"Well that's really a desperate move."

"Love makes you do anything. The very first time I saw her I decided to make any sacrifice and I went to see her with the intention of promising her money if she did what I wanted, but she didn't accept. Before she knew the reason for my visit, she received me charmingly, which encouraged me to begin to speak. But I had just begun to talk to her when she changed her tone, grew stern and seeing that I was persistent, she showed me the door."

"Was this the first time you spoke to her?"

"Yes."

"You've still got a chance. The first and second time, women — especially the married ones — don't accept a proposition. You have to run after them, begin by buying them presents and hang around them, tell them patiently that you love them and not all at once."

"Yes, that's true, but now that I've done it, I can't go back and start again."

"In any case, buy a pearl necklace and take it to her tomorrow. I am sure the necklace will have a great effect."

"Yes, you're right, but you didn't see how fiercely she refused me."

"That's nothing. The harder they are at the beginning, the softer they are later. Do what I say and you'll see."

"I'll try what you say but I don't think it will be successful."

"If it isn't, it means that I know nothing at all about women."

The two friends separated and Richard went straight to a jeweller he knew and told him to show him a pearl necklace.

The jeweller showed him many necklaces and at last

the lovelorn young man chose one of them and bought it provisionally. As he paid the jeweller he said: "If my wife likes it she'll keep it. I've already paid you. If she doesn't like it, I'll bring it back and you'll return my money."

The jeweller agreed, and Richard took the necklace and went home intending to take it to Julietta the following day.

Chapter 11

We'll leave Richard with his necklace and his hopes for the moment, and go back to Julietta's house to see what is about to happen there.

Our readers will certainly remember what Julietta had realised when Maurice had come to say he was in love with her, and how she had sensed that this was her husband's doing. When Richard came and went, straightaway she began once more to suspect that her husband had sent him to test her for a second time. She began to feel very angry and grind her teeth. That night, when her wretched husband came home, she began to shout at him: "Listen, Armand, if you don't trust me, don't have me as your wife. I can't put up any more with your testing. I've told you lots of times that I'm faithful, that no man can deceive me and that I'll never try to sell my husband's honour. What is this madness, sending men to test if I'm faithful?"

"Who sent men?" exclaimed Armand who really had no idea of what had been going on.

"Who else would send men here? It's you! Yesterday it was Maurice. Today it was Richard. Tomorrow we'll see which Tom, Dick or Harry it is."

"Richard? Which Richard?"

"Your friend. The lawyer's son."

"The one with fair hair?"

"Yes, him."

"I swear, Julietta, that I don't know anything about that. If you want the truth, yes, it was I who sent Maurice yesterday, but I don't know anything about Richard."

"So why did he come here? How can he have the cheek to come here and tell me he's in love with me when he hardly knows me?"

"Julietta, I swear on my honour that I don't know anything about it. When did he come?"

"Today."

"And what did he say to you?"

"What would he say? What all you men say to women. 'I love you. I adore you, I'm dying for you' and all the other fancy words designed to deceive us women."

"And what did you say to him?"

"What do you think I said? I told him to come back tomorrow."

"What? What did you say? You invited him to come tomorrow?"

"Are you mad? How could I have said that? And if I did invite him do you think I would tell you? I threw him out on his neck and told him never to dare to come to our house again."

"You did very well. Bravo! I'm beginning to believe you really are a faithful woman."

Armand said this in a very kindly way, but in his heart he began to think of something else, and he went on: "Dear Julietta. Let's not prolong this conversation. I didn't test you, and I don't need to do so. I know you're a chaste woman. But I must tell you that I came home early to tell you I have to go to a meeting this evening for some very important business."

"What important business? Are you going to meet another friend to send him here to test me?"

"No, darling. It's some business that I think will earn me a lot of money."

"If that's the case off you go. Don't be late."

Armand listened to his wife and, impatiently, he left saying to himself: "Here's another chance which I must not neglect. Richard has told my wife he loves her. He's a very clever man and I must allow him to continue to test my wife's fidelity."

He began to walk more quickly and soon he was at the hotel where Richard slept every night.

"Is Sinyor Richard in?" he asked the porter.

"Yes, sir, he's just come in."

"Please tell me his room number."

"Number 14."

Armand ran up the stairs and knocked on the door of number 14.

A voice replied: "Come in". And Armand opened the door and went in.

Richard was sitting on a sofa examining the necklace.

"*Bonsoir*, Richard!" exclaimed Armand as he walked in.

Richard's face changed colour when he saw Julietta's husband. What had he come for? Had his wife said something to him?

Without revealing his thoughts, Richard courteously welcomed him with a handshake.

"Welcome, Armand. To what do I owe the pleasure of this visit? Since you've been married you've completely forgotten about your friends."

"I've forgotten my friends, but you've forgotten that this is my honeymoon. A man who's just married is always thinking about his wife in the first few months."

"Yes, of course. I've not been married so I wouldn't know. In any case. I'm wondering about your visit. So what has made you come and see me one evening during your honeymoon?"

"Yes, I knew you would wonder why I'm here, but I've come to ask a favour."

"A favour? From me? You're richer than me and have more influence than I do. What sort of favour could I do for you?"

"A very great favour."

"A loan?"

"No. Thank God I've got plenty of money."

"So, what then?"

"Listen, Richard. My wife told me you came to my place this morning and you told her that you loved her."

At this, Richard began to tremble but he let Julietta's husband continue.

"Don't tremble and don't be scared. We've all been lads and we all know the power of love. Maybe you saw

70

her at some ball, you fancied her and you fell in love with her. I only want you to tell me the truth. What did she answer?"

"What d'you think she answered? She gave me a negative answer and threw me out."

"Are you telling me the truth?"

"I swear. Absolute truth."

"Well, since it's like that, the favour I want to ask you is to go on trying, but on condition not to betray my trust."

"How? What?"

"What you heard. I want you to continue telling my wife that you love her and see if she gives in."

"But what for?"

"I want to test her!"

"Idiot! You don't test a wife, ever! Once you see that she is faithful, leave things alone. Why provoke her and risk her doing something wrong?"

"I must know if she is really chaste."

"What you're doing is mad. You can't really love your wife."

"I love her very much."

"If you love her, you ought to trust her."

"It's just the opposite. It's because I love her that I'm so jealous."

"Daft idea! You don't play around with a woman like that."

"What's it to you? I want you to test her, the more so because she suspected that I had asked you to do so."

"This is the way to make your life impossible. I really must tell you, it's because I really fell for your wife that I had the nerve to go to your house and tell her I love her. When she said no I lost all hope and I've decided not to knock at that door any more and not to make a real ass of myself... But, since that's what you want, to do you this favour, I'll go back! But you can be quite sure that your wife will not accept my proposition. This is absolutely definite, and I noticed it yesterday."*

"Yes, I know also, but I want to be really sure."

"So, I'll go again tomorrow and I'll tell you what transpires."

"You promise?"

"I promise, dear Armand."

"Right, I'm off."

And Armand stood up, said goodbye to Richard, and left.

---

*Richard visited Julietta that same morning. This is an example of the speed and lack of revision with which this novel was written and printed.

Chapter 12

You can just imagine how happy Richard was when he heard what Armand said about going to see Julietta again. He had been thinking a lot about how he could get to see her without meeting her husband, and worrying that Julietta might tell Armand about his second visit, but Armand's words encouraged him to try his luck again, for a second time, but this time using the necklace. Now he had hopes of success.

Very impatiently, he waited all night and when he saw morning come, he shaved, combed his hair and ran to see Julietta at eleven o'clock.

The beautious Julietta had already forgotten what had happened the day before. It was true that, the previous evening, she had quarrelled with her husband because she had thought that Richard was another friend whom Armand had sent to test her, but when later that night her husband came and talked to her about the matter, he assured that that was not the case. So she relaxed and forgot completely about what Richard had said to her.

So she was amazed to see him come again the following day. She received him rather more coolly and our young Richard, without being at all discouraged, bowed to her and said: "Madame, I beg you to excuse the disturbance that my visit caused yesterday. As I was walking through the jewellers' bazaar I saw a pearl necklace. I liked it and I bought it for you, Madame."

"You troubled yourself for nothing, Sinyor Richard. A pearl necklace cannot buy my honour. I beg you not to try in vain for things that can never be. The answer I gave you yesterday is still the same today. This is the last time I'll tell you, I cannot sell my heart to anyone. It belongs to my husband alone, so I beg you not to come here again because it's of no benefit to you and could bring me a lot of trouble. My husband is very jealous and if by chance he came when you were here, it would be the end of me."

"If your husband leaves you, I will take you."

"Many thanks, Sinyor, but if I were to be transferred from one man to another, it would mean dishonour. The only legacy I received from my late father was family honour, and I must never abandon it."

"I don't know what to say to you, Madame, to answer this obstinacy of yours. I know that women are very tender-hearted when it's a matter of not allowing a young man to die when he is dying for love of them."

"This is where you are quite wrong. Women who give in to someone who wants to die for them, also give in for the present that they are going to get from their lover, or else they are already used to doing so. Go and look for one of them, and she'll very quickly take pity on you."

Richard did not lose heart at this reply and answered boldly: "Could it be, Madame, that you think it's your husband who has sent me to test you and that's why you don't want to trust me? I swear, Madame, that you are quite mistaken. I love you from the bottom of my heart and you're mistaken about everything you're thinking about this."

"Sinyor Richard, don't keep trying to go round and round to see if you can trap me. There's nothing for you here. Please leave. For the last time, I'm asking you in a nice way, but if you persist, I'm going to have to show you the door."

And as she said these words, Julietta added: "And as for the necklace, give it to a woman who will satisfy your desires and not to me."

Richard lost heart completely. He rose, made his farewell to Armand's wife without taking her hand and left.

Chapter 13

When Richard left Julietta's house, he was sad and down-hearted. He had fallen in love with Julietta, and her pretty face had stirred his heart. He walked along like an idiot when suddenly, somebody stopped him, saying: "What did you you do? Were you successful?"

Richard looked up and saw Armand, Julietta's husband.

"You should congratulate yourself, Armand," exclaimed Richard, "your wife is faithful."

"How can you be sure?"

"Even the firmest woman gives in if you give her a pearl necklace. But your wife didn't soften even with that."

"You took her a pearl necklace?"

"That's right."

"And what did she say?"

"She threw it back at me and said: 'if you talk to me about this again I shan't even look at you.' I carried on but she threw me out on my neck."

"So what are you going to do now? Aren't you going to come to my house any more?"

"How can I come? This time she threw me out verbally, but the next time she'll use a stick. You know, Armand, that I was always a lad who hung around with women and tried to get them into bed. I've always been successful until now. I assure you you should congratulate yourself on having a faithful wife."

Armand began to think of the necklace. He didn't want to believe what Richard had said.

Richard went on: "Go home, Armand, go home, and be really happy. Your wife is a chaste woman!"

Armand departed, leaving Richard to sigh with remorse and exclaim to himself: "I, Richard, not to be able to have the only woman that I've ever loved in my life!"

And he continued walking, head down, thinking.

Suddenly a voice roused him from his thoughts. It was Giacomo, his friend, who woke him up as he called out: "What happened, Richard? Was my advice useful?"

"No, not at all, dear friend, neither the necklace, nor my entreaties nor my tears had any effect on her."

"Didn't you persist?"

"More than you think. But she showed me the door and told me not to come again."

Giacomo was very surprised and asked: "Can you introduce me to this woman?"

"How can I introduce you to her if she told me not to go there again?"

"I've only got to see her once and I'm sure I can get her into bed."

This reply intrigued Richard, who had just had an idea, and he hurriedly replied: "Look, Giacomo, beside the love I have for this woman, I'm also angry, I mean I want revenge. I can't introduce you to her, but there's a way that you can see her and even go there two or three times."

"What's that?"

"I'll tell you. When you advised me to buy a necklace, I did so straightaway and I went home to examine it. Just as I was counting the pearls, I saw Julietta's husband come into my room. You can imagine my alarm. I was sure he was coming to reproach me for my behaviour towards his wife, but I was astonished when I saw that he was coming for exactly the opposite reason. He asked me to continue to go to his house because he wanted to test his wife's love. I protested at first, but then I accepted the mission. And today precisely, he's going to come at midday for the answer and find out what I did. If you come with me, I'll tell him I got nowhere and I'll introduce you as being much more capable than me. I'm sure he'll be glad to accept and he himself will introduce you to his wife."

"That's a good idea. Let's go straight to the house and if Armand agrees to let me test his wife's fidelity, I'll show you how to trap a woman, however obstinate she is."

Arm in arm the two friends began to walk to Richard's house.

To their great surprise, Armand was already waiting at the door and the colour of his face changed when he saw Richard arriving with another friend.

Richard saw this at once, but he didn't hesitate to walk up and say: "I was expecting to see you, Sinyor Armand. *Buon Giorno**. It looks as though Heaven wants to help you in the plan that you've in mind."

Armand was uncomfortable at what Richard was saying, not wanting the friend he had with him to learn what it was all about. Richard continued: "First of all, my dear Armand, let me introduce my friend Sinyor Giacomo, a very able young man who can be very useful to you in what you want to know."

Armand was very surprised and replied: "Does he know about our business?"

"Yes, I had to tell him because the truth is that I couldn't get anywhere with it."

"You weren't successful? What did she say?"

"Still a negative answer, and she wasn't far from throwing me out of the door."

"And what can Sinyor Giacomo do?"

"Let's go inside. We'll be more comfortable speaking there."

The three men went inside. Richard invited them to sit and then sat down himself, addressing himself to Armand in these words: "Look, Armand, the first time I told your wife I loved her, she wouldn't listen and I lost hope completely and didn't intend to go to see her again. By chance I met Giacomo and told him about how much I loved Julietta. He advised me to buy a pearl necklace and

---

*The presence of wealthy Italian families in the Eastern Sephardi led to the occasional use of expressions in that language.

go again. I bought one for her, I took it to her, but the answer was the same, always negative and a categorical refusal and she threw me out of the house."

"But, just like the first time, I confided in Giacomo again and he called me an ass. He said that if I introduced him to that woman he could trap her the first time he met her or at least at the second. As soon as he said that, I thought of you. All you need to do is take him to your house once and introduce him to your wife. The rest is up to him."

Armand began to think as he said to himself: "This man prides himself on being very clever and he is sure to seduce my wife. Yes, it's true that she threw two hopeful lovers out of the house, but if she weakens finally, she's only flesh and bone and can certainly be seduced."

He though about this over and over again but the desire to be sure of his wife's fidelity refused to leave and he wanted very much to try again. He looked up and speaking to Giacomo said: "You think you can seduce a woman who glorifies in her chastity?"

"Yes, Sinyor Armand."

"And what do you want me to do for this?"

"Just take me to your house for lunch once and introduce me to you wife. The rest is up to me. But you must pay me five hundred francs for this service."

"Five hundred francs? What are you selling which is worth so much?"

"My skill, Sinyor Armand."

"And if you don't get anywhere?"

"Then you don't give me anything."

"Knock something off the price, please. Five hundred francs is very dear."

"I'll do something better. Show me your wife once, and then look at each other. I'll be able to tell you if she can be seduced or not."

"That's better. I agree."

"Right, now, tonight, when you go home, tell your wife that you've received a telegram from one of your friends in London, a very dear friend called Lord George Frodel. He will arrive tomorrow morning and you've got to entertain him to lunch at home. The rest is up to me."

"We agree, then. I'm going home now to tell my wife to begin preparations for lunch tomorrow. Tomorrow at 11 o'clock, meet me here. I'll take you to my place and we'll see just how able you are."

The two new friends shook hands to show they were in agreement and said goodbye.

Armand went straight home.

Chapter 15
(as numbered in the original, it should be 14)

When Armand left Richard's house he was very happy. His conversation with Giacomo made him believe that he was going to be able to discover what he wanted to learn. He walked home briskly, to his wife's great surprise.

"What is it, Armand. Why have you come home in the middle of the day?"

"I've got to. I've just received a telegram from London from one of my closest friends, Lord George Frodel, with whom we do a great deal of business every month. He tells me he's left London to come and see me and that he'll be here tomorrow morning. So I had to run home to tell you to start making preparations now because when he arrives tomorrow he must have lunch with us."

"Oh dear!" said the woman, "Don't you know how much I dislike having guests here, particularly when it's a foreigner?"

"True, you know I try much more than I need not to bring people here, but this lord, with whom I do a lot of business, well, I must bring him here."

"All the same, I can't do anything. Go to a big restaurant, order the dishes you want them to serve to the people who are coming to visit us, and don't bother me."

"There nobody coming except the lord."

"All right then, do what you like, I can't be bothered."

"I'll arrange things with pleasure. You don't have to go to any trouble. But... I think I can ask you just to arrange the furniture here a little."

"Men don't have anything to do with household matters. I know what I have to do. Your honour is my honour."

"Right. Do as you like. I'm off." And he kissed his wife goodbye as he did every day and left.

Chapter 16

When Giacomo found himself alone with Maurice*, he began to rub his hands together, and with a sneer on his face he began to tease Maurice, saying: "Now you're going to see how I'll get what I want! You're useless and you don't know how to handle a woman."

"You can't say anything if you don't see her and you don't manage to seduce her."

"I know how good I am and I've been around a bit."

"We'll speak again tomorrow evening."

They began talking about this and that and arranged to meet that night at the theatre. They spent the whole night in having a good time and waited impatiently for the morning to come. They slept for a couple of hours and got up for a coffee and waited for Armand. He hadn't slept that night either. He was very impatient and as soon as dawn came out he went to the street. But he was embarrassed to go so early so he walked about for close on an hour and then went straight to Maurice's house, just when they had got up and were having their morning coffee.

"Bravo, Armand," said Maurice. "You now how to choose the moment. Just when the coffee is on the table you make an appearance. Have you had yours yet?"

"I've had three coffees already."

"So have a fourth and tell us what's you've done."

"What I've done? I told my wife that Lord George Frodel is coming from London to visit me and that I do lots of business with him, so I'm bringing him to lunch at my place today. She accepted with pleasure. What's the time?"

Maurice looked and said:

---

*This is another example of the speed and lack of revision of this novel. Giacano is talking to Richard, not Maurice.

"Half-past ten."

"Let's wait another half hour and then take a cab and go."

Chapter 17

You can just imagine Giacomo and Armand's impatience for eleven o'clock to come for them to set off. Armand was more restless than Giacomo. At last the clock on the wall chimed eleven and Armand, taking Giacomo by the arm, left Maurice's house. They hired a luxurious motor car and had themselves driven to Armand's home.

Julietta was waiting for them, dressed in a pink *robe de chambre* which made her look even more beautiful and, with a greeting such as high society ladies give, she received her husband and his guest.

"Madame Armand," said Julietta's husband, "may I introduce Lord Frodel?"

"I am most honoured to meet you, Madame," said Giacomo as he took her hand.

Having made the introductions, they moved into the main reception room, where they were offered sweet things. After the usual polite phrases, some business talk, and this and that, they went in to lunch. Here, Sinyor Armand began to compliment Giacomo by telling his wife to sit beside him, but Giacomo whispered hastily to him "sit her opposite me."

The meal was served in a very elegant way. The bottles of champagne danced from hand to hand as each drank to the health of the other. Armand toasted the false Lord Frodel and when Giacomo's turn came, he said: "If Sinyor Armand does not object, I want to toast Sinyora Julietta to thank her for the kind way she has received me in her home."

"This is merely my duty. A wife ought to honour her husband and his friends also."

"I thank you, Madame, for an honour I do not deserve."

At that moment, Armand left the room to give orders to bring in the fruit, and Giacomo went on: "I swear, Madame, that if I had known that Armand had a wife of such rare beauty, I would have come here six months earlier."

Julietta smiled gently and said to herself: "This lord looks like another one of those we already know."

Then they served the fruit. Then they talked about various matters, and Giacomo said in a serious tone: "Armand, it's time we should be off. We've got a lot of things to discuss."

"Yes, let's go."

They stood up and Giacomo, with an elegant bow, took Julietta's hand and drew it to his lips. He withdrew bowing once more. They left and got into the motor car which was awaiting them.

Chapter 18

Once in the street, Armand asked: "Well Giacomo, am I right to be jealous?"

"Certainly. You are fortunate to have a wife of rare beauty, and you're right to want to be sure that she is faithful. In any case, I'll do everything I can to satisfy you, beginning tomorrow. I'll visit Julietta and try to seduce her."

The motor car brought them back to Richard's house. Armand went to his business and Giacomo went in to visit his friend. The latter was expecting him and when he saw him come his eyes shone as he asked: "Well, Giacomo. What did you think of Julietta?"

"*Charmante*! Women as beautiful as that are very rare. I really liked her and I'm sure I won't fail like you did."

"That's exactly what I said when Maurice praised her to me, but when I was with her I saw that she's not the sort of woman you can play around with. She's chaste."

"We'll see!"

"If you are successful in this I promise to invite you to lunch and spend 2000 francs."

Giacomo began to smile and replied: "No woman escapes me if I fancy her. I've been invited to dine with them tonight and from tomorrow you'll see what Giacomo is capable of."

The two friends occupied the day in this and that. That evening Armand came again to take Giacomo to his home. This time Julietta's hopeful new lover came in another suit, another hat, gloves of another colour and different rings on his fingers. With all this luxury he intended to show Julietta that he was very rich.

When Armand and Giacomo arrived, Julietta welcomed her husband's friend warmly, as he expected and, as her took her hand, he didn't hesitate to say: "Does your warm welcome really come from your heart?"

Julietta looked at him and replied gravely.

"Of course. My husband's friends are always welcome here."

They went into the drawing-room and the conversation began. Giacomo did not take his eyes off Julietta, and the lady was aware of it and lowered her glance and said to herself: "He's one of those men..."

The meal was ready. They went in to eat and the bottles of champagne began to dance a polka around the table.

Here again, Giacomo found the occasion to clink glasses with Julietta and every time the glasses clinked he said his charming phrases, intended to show Julietta that he liked her.

Finally the meal came to an end and Giacomo invited husband and wife to accompany him to the theatre, where a box had been reserved earlier that day.

The invitation was accepted, the motor car was waiting at the door and the three got in. As courtesy requires, Armand had to seat Giacomo next to his wife, while he sat in front.

This again was a chance for Giacomo to say what he felt. He had only just sat next to Julietta when he whispered in her ear: "Madame, how lucky I am to have you sitting beside me!"

Julietta did not reply, and Giacomo began to suspect the worst, as he said to himself: "This is going to be a hard nut to crack."

Finally they arrived at the theatre.

Armand's *mazal* had it that night they were putting on the play called *The Jealous Husband*. It was a play which showed how a husband who loved his wife deeply, was very jealous of her, watched her like a hawk, and at the same time adored her. They were always having rows because of his jealousy. Not having any children, the woman grew weary of her husband, ran away and abandoned him.

The play made Armand's heart beat fiercely, but it also gave a great weapon to Giacomo to begin to speak in these words: "What do you think of the play, Madame? Who is right, the husband or the wife?"

"Neither the husband nor the wife, because even though a husband is jealous, the wife should not sell her honour, which is the only thing a wife has."

This reply was not what Giacomo wanted to hear, but he had to bite his tongue and keep silent for the moment.

Finally the play finished. Armand and Julietta went home and Giacomo went back to his hotel to sleep.

Chapter 19

When Giacomo left Armand and Julietta he went to the hotel and, throwing himself on the bed, began to think about what he should to succeed in what he wanted. He found the nut very hard to crack and was beginning to admit to himself that Richard was right. That night he could not sleep and, next morning, as soon as he rose, he brought his hand down hard on the table.

"There's no alternative... everything is hard at the beginning but once you start it gets easier as you go along."

He dressed, left, had a coffee, had himself shaved and waited impatiently in the café for the clock to read half-past ten. When he saw the clock on the wall read ten he stood up and began to walk at a resolute pace. At exactly half past ten Giacomo was at the door of Armand's house. He knocked, the servant opened the door, recognised him at once and asked him to come in.

"Is Sinyor Armand in?" he asked.

"No, Sinyor."

"And Madame?"

"Madame is dressing and about to go out."

"Please tell her I am here."

The servant went and came back saying that she could not receive guests when her husband was not there. "In any case, since you have come to see Sinyor Armand, Madame said that you can come back at lunch time when he will be at home."

You can imagine how disappointed Giacomo was as he said to himself: "Richard was luckier than me. He was fortunate enough to be received once or twice here, when the husband wasn't here, but I haven't even had that much luck."

He was thinking this in the patio, when suddenly Julietta came down the stairs dressed and with her hat, ready to leave. Seeing Giacomo standing in the patio, looking pensive, she smiled and said: "Please excuse me, Sinyor Lord, for not receiving you. I'm in a hurry to go and visit a friend of mine whom I've arranged to meet at eleven and it's a quarter to already."

"You are right, Madame, but I wanted to speak to you about something very impor..."

"I know what you want to talk about. In fact that's exactly why I didn't want to receive you."

"How can you know without my telling you?"

"You don't need to say anything, Sinyor Lord. The way you looked at me at dinner yesterday and in the theatre is quite enough for me to understand your intentions. In any case, don't waste your time in what is pointless. I'm not one of those bold women you meet, who know how to organise their budgets with the help of presents from gentlemen friends. I must have just one lover and I have him already. It's my husband."

"But Madame, you are making an assumption before I have even ventured to speak to you."

"There's no need for you to say anything. I understand you completely."

Giacomo was about to continue, but Julietta did not let him. She left him with the words on his tongue and walked out of the house... The motor car was awaiting her, she climbed in and told the driver where he was to go.

Giacomo was left standing there open-mouthed, as women say. He began to think and exclaimed suddenly.

"I'm going to see the husband. I'm going to come back to lunch with him, then I'll tell him to leave the house without telling his wife, and then we'll see what he does."

He left Armand's house and went straight to Armand's office. He found him writing and, cheerfully wishing him good morning, he walked in and shook his hand.

"Oh! *Buon giorno*," exclaimed Armand. "Welcome. What's new?"

"Nothing. Your wife wouldn't invite me in although I

insisted on having a few words with her. She said she was very busy and, leaving me with the words on my tongue, she went to visit somebody and she left me standing at the street door and said: 'If you want to talk to me, come at noon with my husband.'"

"That's no good," exclaimed Armand. "If I'm there you won't be able to say anything."

"True, but I thought of something else. At noon we'll go back to your house together and as soon as you finish eating, you must leave without telling her, and when I'm alone with her I'll be able to play my part perfectly."

"That's a good idea!" Armand looked at the time and seeing that it was almost half-past eleven, he said: "Let's go now. You'll have half an hour more to talk to my wife and this will let you get to know her better."

"But your wife isn't at home. She said she had to meet a friend at eleven so she's been out for barely half an hour."

"It doesn't matter. Let's go. We may meet her. You know, my wife is very sharp. It's very possible that, when she overheard that you had come to see her, she dressed specifically to show that she was going out, and then came back. Come on, you'll see that I'm right."

They left, called a taxi and were driven to Armand's place.

Chapter 20

This time Armand's judgement had failed him. Julietta had gone to visit a friend called Madame Clotilde, an old schoolfriend to whom she was very close. Madame Clotilde welcomed her warmly and noticed that Julietta was very pensive and looked sad.

"Dear Julietta, what's the matter?" asked Clotilde.

"I don't even know what's the matter. I'm very happy but the only problem is that my husband is very jealous."

"All husbands are jealous."

"But not like mine. The wretch is bringing men to see if I'll deceive him. I'm only human. Since our wedding, he's already brought four or five men to the house to see if they can seduce me. I refused them all but, God forbid, some devil might charm me and, I assure you, I don't want to deceive my husband."

"Don't be silly. Husbands like that deserve to be deceived."

"No, my dear, my honour comes first. I'm pregnant and I don't want people to think the baby is a bastard."

"Well, then, you'll have to convince him that he's wrong."

"I've talked to him a lot but he doesn't want to understand."

Hardly had Julietta uttered that last sentence when an idea occurred to her and she exclaimed: "I've got it! I swear, Clotilde, I'm going to teach him a good lesson. You'll see if I don't."

The two friends began to talk of this and that, and at exactly ten minutes to twelve, Julietta stood up to say goodbye to her friend. By midday exactly Armand's wife was back home. She was not at all surprised to see Giacomo there in her husband's company.

"Welcome, Sinyor Giacomo, now you can say everything you want."

Giacomo was very embarrassed because it was not in front of the husband that the conversation was meant to take place. He looked down and indicated with a movement of his lips that Juliet should say nothing in front of her husband.

Armand's wife smiled as she looked at him with one of those glances which pierce a man's heart. The meal was ready and the three went in to eat at once.

The first course was the soup.

"I've never had soup like this before," said Giacomo, "blessed be the hand that made it."

The second course was chicken. Julietta herself served her guests and carefully arranged for herself to have the piece with the wishbone. Then they began to eat and when Julietta came to the wishbone she said to her husband.

"Armand, do you want to play *Yades*?"

"What's the forfeit?"

"Either you buy me a dress, or I buy you a coat."

"Agreed. And husband and wife split the wishbone."*

Then came rice and dessert. Armand finished and found a moment to leave when his wife was out of the room. He left, leaving Giacomo alone with her.

Yades requires one person to pay a forfeit if he or she takes something offered by the other without uttering the word "*Yades*" — see introduction.

Chapter 21

You can imagine how happy Giacomo was to find himself alone with Julietta. She, not knowing that her husband had left, came and sat at the table again. Seeing Giacomo alone, she thought that her husband had gone to brush his teeth, so she sat down again opposite Giacomo. Giacomo rubbed his hands together as he lost no time in beginning to speak.

"Madame, as you see, I did not fail to carry out your orders and I came with your husband who is not here now. Will you please allow me to say a few words to you?"

Julietta looked straight at Giacomo, smiled and said: "I would like you to tell me if my husband asked you to test my fidelity."

"Madame, I swear I don't know what you are talking about."

"So, what do you want to talk to me about?"

"To ask your pity, Madame. Since the very first moment I saw you, I don't know what's been wrong with me, Madame. My heart is racing, my mind is falling to pieces, and to tell you the truth, Madame, though I've known many women, this is the first time I've begun to understand what love really is."

"You're repeating the same words that all you men say when they want to trap some woman."

"I swear I'm not, Madame. Have pity on me. A refusal on your part would be a death sentence for me."

Julietta began to think as Giacomo went on. "Madame, I beg you, I implore you, trust me. I love you!"

And as he uttered these words Giacomo threw himself on his knees in front of Armand's wife, and continued: "Madame, take pity!"

Julietta raised Giacomo off his knees, saying: "You men are such liars that a woman can't even believe one who is telling the truth. I rather like you, but I'm scared you might be a spy sent by my husband."

"Madame, you're mistaken. I swear by what I hold most sacred in life, I love you pure-heartedly and there's no spying about it. On the contrary, if you agree to leave your husband, I am ready to make you my wife and I promise you'll have a life like no other woman."

"Give me until tomorrow midday to think about it. Come and have lunch here with my husband as you did today, on condition that as soon as you finish eating you get up to leave. If I decide to love you, I'll go with you to the patio and I'll shut you in a cupboard until my husband leaves. If you see that I don't leave with you it means I do not want to accept your offer, so don't venture to come to my house again."

"But, Madame, I beg you to give me some hope."

"You can count on an affirmative rather than a negative answer."

"Thank you, Madame, but please give me something on account of my love for you."

"Not today, I'm not even going to give you my hand when you go. My husband may very well have hidden in some corner to see us talking."

Giacomo stood up at once and with some difficulty grasped Julietta's hand and took it to his lips. Then he left, happy to have achieved the first part of his aim.

"I shan't say anything to Armand," he said to himself, "because if I manage to seduce Julietta, she'll be available every day and her husband mustn't know."

He went down to the patio very happily and began to look for a cupboard to hide in the next day. Suddenly Armand appeared and asked him.

"Well, Giacomo, what happened?"

"Nothing. Your wife is faithful. In any case I'm coming for lunch tomorrow. If I'm successful then, well and good, but if not, it means that no woman is as chaste as your wife."

And that is how Giacomo deceived his friend, as he waited impatiently for the next day to come. Finally, it arrived, and Giacomo, accompanied by the husband, came once more for lunch at Julietta's house.

The mistress of the house welcomed him warmly, with a joy on her face that she had not expressed before, in order to give him to understand that she agreed with what they had said the previous day.

Giacomo looked at her in such as way as to ask if Julietta had made a decision in his favour, and with a movement of her eyebrows Julietta replied that she had, and this delighted the guest.

Having finished lunch, Giacomo stood up to take his leave. Julietta went with him to the patio and, opening a large cupboard, she ushered him inside and locked the door behind him. Then she came back to the table as if nothing had happened.

Armand, for his part, made as if to leave but his wife stopped him, saying: "Sit down, Armand, I've got something to say to you."

"But I'm busy, let it wait until tonight."

"No, Armand, here and now I want you to tell me that this behaviour of yours has got to finish. You're bringing one man after the other to test me, but you don't realise that maybe I'll like one of them one day and he will seduce me."

"I haven't brought anyone to try to seduce you."

"Liar! You've brought many, and Giacomo is the latest one!"

"Giacomo! I brought Giacomo to test you?"

"Yes, and the proof is that, without saying anything to you, he made his declaration of love and he told me that if I did what he wanted he'd tell me a secret."

"And what did you do?"

"The truth is, Armand, that I refused all the others' propositions, but I couldn't refuse Giacomo. He touched my heart and I promised him I would do what he wanted today."

"You're going to give him what he wants today?... You mean after I leave?"

95

"Exactly."

"Is Giacomo going to come back here?"

"He's here already, he doesn't have to come."

"Where is he?"

"I put him in the cupboard in the patio."

Armand went red with anger and said to himself: "The wretch. He's going to seduce my wife without telling me. And he shouted as he ran to the patio:

"I'll kill the wretch!"

"Why are you running?" exclaimed his wife. "I've got the key to the cupboard. How are you going to open it?"

And she gave him the key, but as soon as he took it she exclaimed: *"Yades*! I've won the forfeit, but not only the dress you promised. You've also got to give up your suspicions about me. If I really wanted to hide my lover, I would know how to do it without you suspecting anything. In any case, if you want to make sure, go and open the cupboard and you'll find him inside."

Armand went and to his great surprise he found Giacomo in the cupboard. Giacomo was also amazed to see Armand open the cupboard rather than Julietta, as he had hoped.

This lesson served to teach Sinyor Armand not to be jealous of his wife, while Sinyor Giacomo went back to his room with with his tail between his legs, tricked by the woman whom he had tried to trick.

From that day on, husband and wife lived very contentedly, and whenever they found a wishbone in the chicken, Armand was afraid to play *Yades*, remembering the dress and the guest in the cupboard.

THE END

Prologo

En 1492, los Reyes Católicos, Isabel de Castilla y Fernando de Aragón, decretaron la expulsión de España de todos aquellos judíos que, después de más de un siglo de presiones, se negaban aún a convertirse al catolicismo. Aunque muchos judíos se bautizaron, decenas de miles aceptaron la alternativa, y después de más de un milenio de présencia en España, emigraron al imperio otomano, el cual en 1453 había tomado Constantinopla, capital cristiana del Oriente.

En épocas siguientes, judíos españoles que habían pasado antes por Portugal, Italia o Africa del Norte, vinieron a instalarse en ciudades tales como Belgrado, Sarayevo, Sofía, Salónica, Constantinopla, Esmirna, Alepo, Tsefat, Tiberiades, Jerusalén, Hebrón, El Cairo y Alejandría, donde mantuvieron su lengua y sus costumbres españolas. En su apogeo a mediados del siglo XIX, la población judía hispanohablante del imperio llegaba a trescientos mil.

Comenzando hacia finales del siglo XIX, la emigración, principalmente a la Europa occidental y al continente americano, comenzó a reducir el tamaño de la población hispanófona oriental. Más tarde, en las naciones independientes surgidas con la desintegración en 1918 del imperio turco, los nacionalismos fueron absorbiendo la cultura judía. En la guerra de 1939-1945, la ocupación alemana de los balcanes, de Grecia y de la isla de Rodas, seguida de las deportaciones y asesinatos en masa de los judíos, completó la destrucción de aquellas antiguas comunidades.

Después de la guerra, la mayoría de los judíos hispanófonos sobrevivientes se mudaron a la Europa Occidental o al continente americano, mientras que el establecimiento en 1948 del Estado de Israel aumentó sensiblemente la población de judíos españoles o sefardíes que desde hacía siglos vivían en Palestina.

La lengua de los sefardíes era el castellano de 1492, el cual experimentó los cambios naturales del tiempo, aceptando en su léxico muchas palabras turcas. Sin embargo, el crecimiento de los nacionalismos después del colapso en 1918 del imperio multilingüe turco, junto con la influencia poderosa del francés ejercida sobre las tres generaciones de sefardíes formadas en los colegios de la *Alliance Israélite Universelle*, ya estaban, para los años treinta, debilitando el empleo del español. Entre los que emigraron, en Estados Unidos todos tuvieron que aprender inglés — lo cual no había sucedido en el imperio otomano con el turco, que pocos sefardíes sabían —. En los países de habla española los sefardíes adoptaron muy fácil y casi inconscientemente el castellano moderno, mientras en Israel se impuso el hebreo. Por lo tanto se ha reducido probablemente a cero el número de personas para quienes el español de Oriente es el idioma principal, mientras pocos son capaces de leerlo en el alfabeto hebreo en el cual tradicionalmente se escribía.

El español sefardí de Oriente es llamado a menudo *Ladino*, aunque algunos especialistas prefieren llamarlo *judeo-español*, limitando el uso del vocablo *ladino* a describir la traducción literal, siguiendo la sintaxis hebrea, de los textos bíblicos y litúrgicos. Los que hablan esta lengua la llaman sencillamente lo que es — *español* —, por lo cual en el hebreo israelí se llama *españolit* en contraste con *sefardit*: castellano de España y de Latinoamérica.

Existe gran interés en mantener el conocimiento y el empleo de este idioma en peligro. Se editan, en particular, poesías, aunque en el alfabeto romano introducido hacia finales de los 1920 cuando Kemal Atatürk lo impuso sobre la lengua turca. Se celebran congresos académicos, se editan artículos especializados, mientras un fórum en el *Web* llamado *Ladinokomunita* hace circular diariamente grandes cantidades de mensajes entre sus más de mil miembros.

De vez en cuando, en España, en Turquía y en otras partes se publican ediciones modernas de la literatura judeo-española*. En Israel, la Autoridad Nacional del Ladino protege la lengua, mientras las universidades fomentan el estudio del ladino y su literatura. En Francia hay una cátedra dedicada al ladino, enseñado en el INALCO *(Institut National pour les Langues et Civilisations Orientales)*, mientras en España la sección del *Consejo Nacional de Investigación Científica* dedicada al hebreo abriga una unidad que alienta la investigación sobre el español sefardí. Florecen grupos de investigación en Suiza y trabajan investigadores autonómos en Alemania, Italia, Bulgaria, el Canadá y Estados Unidos.

La finalidad de este libro es introducir a los lectores, anglófonos e hispanófonos, a un aspecto de la cultura judía que suele despertar una curiosidad poco satisfecha y que no debería quedar descuidado. Por esto, el libro ofrece una breve introducción en inglés y en castellano a la literatura judeo-española, y específicamente a la novela. La parte principal consiste en una traducción al inglés de la novela *La mužer† onesta*, escrita por Eliya Karmona, uno de los más conocidos y más prolíficos autores de su época, editada en Constantinopla en el año hebreo 5685 (1924 o 1925), y una transliteración de la novela desde el alfabeto hebreo al romano, siguiendo convenciones ortográficas cuyo fin es reflejar la pronunciación del ladino. Hemos añadido unas notas para clarificar la significación de palabras que o no existen en el castellano de hoy, o son galicismos o palabras turcas.

---

*Empleamos indistintamente los términos *ladino* y *judeoespañol* aunque reconocemos que la palabra *ladino* significa la traducción literal al español desde el hebreo bíblico, rabínico o litúrgico, y que las personas que hablan el idioma en cuestión suelen llamarlo o "espanyol" o "ǧudiyo". De vez en cuando,como variación, decimos "lengua sefardí" o "español sefardí".

†Véase una explicación del sistema ortográfico empleado per el español sefardí, al principio de nuestra transliteración.

Doy sentidas gracias a mi editor, Ross Bradshaw, de Five Leaves Publications, por su interés y su constante apoyo, al congreso de Estudios Judeo-Españoles celebrado cada dos años en el Queen Mary College de la Universidad de Londres, a su organizadora la Dra. Hilary Pomeroy, a Elena Romero del CSIC en Madrid, a Pilar Romeu de Barcelona, a Gaëlle Collin de la *Alliance* en París y al profesor Dov Hakohen del Instituto Ben-Zvi para el Estudio de los Judíos de Oriente, ubicado en Jerusalén, y a Leon Yudkin, especialista en literatura hebrea y yídica, todos los cuales me han ofrecido aliento y ayuda.

Descubrí *La mužer onesta* en el inventorio de obras en ladino preservadas en la *British Library*, redactado por la jefa de la sección de material judío y hebreo, Ilana Tahan. Ojalá se produzcan en otras bibliotecas catálogos semejantes, herramientas valiosas para los investigadores de esta manifestación de una noble cultura judía y española.

Michael Alpert
Londres, agosto de 2008

Introduccion

Orígenes de la Novela Judeo-Española[1]

El *corpus* de la literatura judeo-española totaliza unos tres mil títulos, que comprenden Biblias, literatura rabínica, liturgia, prensa, novelas, teatro y poesía[2] Sin más pretexto que el de ofrecer una breve contextualización al tema de la novela en caracteres hebreos o *aljamiado*, diremos que los judíos que iban llegando a diversos centros tras su expulsión de España en 1492, principalmente en el imperio otomano, trajeron consigo el arte de imprimir. Hasta el siglo XIX, sin embargo, imprimieron sólo obras religiosas y para-religiosas en hebreo.

Excepcionalmente, en el siglo XVI se editaron en español aljamiado algunas obras de tema religioso, para contribuir a la reabsorción al judaismo de los conversos que llegaban desde la Península. Tales obras incluyen Biblias, libros de oraciones, la narrativa o *Hagadá* del Exodo, leída en la comida familiar para celebrar la Pascua. La mayoría de esta literatura se tradujo literalmente, siguiendo la sintaxis hebrea. Esta "lengua-calco" es la que propiamente se llama "ladino".

La más célebre de todas las obras religiosas judeo-españolas es el *Me'am Lo'ez* ("de un pueblo de lengua extranjera", cita del libro de los *Salmos* [xiv,i], editado en Constantinopla 1730-1777), compuesto por el rabino Ya'akov Juli (1690-1732). Se trata de una obra basada en las Escrituras, que incluye obervaciones legales y morales. Juli completó su comentario sobre el *Génesis*. Otras autoridades rabínicas continuaron la obra, con el fin de ofrecer unas enseñanzas en una lengua accesible, con la máxima claridad, basada en una exposición vivaz con el fin de atraer el interés y la comprensión de sus lectores, los cuales no entendían bien ni el hebreo ni el hebreo ladinado. La mayor parte de las familias hispanoparlantes de Oriente poseían un tomo o por lo menos algunas hojas sueltas de este compendio, y de allí vino la tradición de leer (*meldar*) en alta voz, probablemente los sábados por la tarde. La lectura ofrecía un modelo para la futura lectora de periódicos y novelas[3]. Como escribió el rabino Juli en la Introducción a su comentario:

> agora, cuando viene la presona de la botica y tanbien dia de šabat [sábado] y mo'ed [festivo] que no hay que hacer, ya se embebece en este libro y melda [lee][4] la licion que le place.

La sabiduría rabínica presentada como un discurso no-élite ofrecía un modelo y una legitimización de la presentación en ladino de la literatura europea y, últimamente, de la creación original en la lengua de los lectores.[5]

Occidentalizacion, Periódicos y Novelas

El impulso de emplear la lengua sefardí para escribir y leer narrativa nació con la creación en Oriente de una prensa en ladino. Empezando en 1853 con *La Luž de Israel*, hubo decenas de títulos, aunque muchos de ellos de corta vida. Entre los de vida más larga se cuentan *La Buena Esperanza* (1871-1922) y *El Meseret* (1897-1920) de Esmirna, *La Epoka* de Salónica y de Constantinopla (1875-1920), *El Telégrafo* (1886-1930), *El Tyempo* (1872-1930), y el humorístico *El Ǧugeton* que Elía Karmona publicó desde 1908 hasta 1930[6]. Gran parte de las novelas vieron la luz en la forma de capítulos en estos periódicos.

El auge del periodismo y de la novela en lengua sefardí, con su momento cumbre entre 1880 y 1930, sucedió contra el fondo de la decadencia del imperio otomán al alimón con el crecimiento del nacionalismo de sus partes constituyentes[7] y reflejando el eco de la Ilustración judía o *Haskalá*. El florecimiento de la producción laica en ladino duró poco más de medio siglo, terminando con la decadencia de la misma lengua, con la imposición en Turquía del alfabeto romano, el crecimiento de los nacional-ismos turco, griego y búlgaro, y en los años 1940 el asesinato en masa por los nazis de comunidades hispanó-fonas de Grecia, Yugoeslavia y otras partes. Tales comunidades en todo caso habían sido debilitadas y espar-cidas antes por las emigraciones, principalmente de gente joven.

La occidentalización de los judíos orientales se debió a la llegada desde los 1860 de las escuelas de la *Alliance Israélite Universelle*[8]. Para 1925, cuando se editó *La mužer onesta*, después de un par de generaciones imbuí-das de valores occidentales, la población lectora leía literatura europea, mayormente francesa, en versiones judeo-españolas traducidas, imitadas, o adaptadas. En esto los judíos no diferían de sus vecinos, ya que la novela turca, en efecto, empieza con traducciones de *Les Misérables*, de Victor Hugo, y *Robinson Crusoe* del irlandés Defoe[9]. A mediados del siglo diecinueve empeza-ban a salir novelas y traducciones en armenio, griego y búlgaro, mientras el número de librerías en Constan-tinopla iba en aumento. En efecto, el contexto de escribir una novela en ladino era semejante al de otras lenguas minoritarias del imperio otomano — búlgaro, griego, armenio y turco mismo, donde la palabra *literatura* se refería anteriormente a textos religiosos. Como ya comentaba Joseph Nehama en su *Histoire des Israélites de Salonique*, de 1936.

On ne commence à se préoccuper de la masse à demi-lettrée que lorsque les écoles ont ouvert une brèche dans les remparts dont s'entoure le fanatisme[10]

La Novela Judeo-Espanola

El ladino no gozaba de alto estatus social. Sin embargo la inmensa mayoría de los judíos de Constantinopla, Salonica, Esmirna y las ciudades de la región lo empleaban. Era el idioma de la instrucción religiosa y había existido, como se ha visto, una tradición ya arraigada de editar en judeo-español material religioso y textos parareligiosos leídos no sólo por hombres, sino por mujeres también. A pesar de los ataques sufridos por el ladino, hasta la década de los 1930 el medio diario de comunicación de la inmensa mayoría de los judíos de los Balcanes y de Turquía era el español sefardí. Los autores no tenían alternativa a emplear el ladino si deseaban alcanzar al público. No existían publicaciones laicas en hebreo en comparación con las revistas y libros que salían en Rusia y Polonia[11]. Es también paradójico que las mismas escuelas de la *Alliance*, pese a sus esfuerzos para suprimir el ladino, al cual llamaban

"jargon bâtard incapable de rendre les nuances, peu fait pour exprimer des idées délicates ou élevées"[12]

produjeron los mismos intelectuales cuya producción cultural iba a emplear el judeo-español tan desdeñado. En efecto, la *Alliance* estimulaba la curiosidad intelectual y por lo tanto la lectura. Y pese a que hubo poco interés desde España, y aunque los mismos sefardíes tampoco tenían gran interés por España mientras, en un galicismo galopante, sustituían parte de sus lexis castellano por palabras francesas, sin embargo, entre la segunda mitad del siglo XIX y la primera guerra mundial hubo una explosión de prensa y de creatividad literaria en la lengua de los sefardíes hispanoparlantes de Oriente.[13]

Para el año 1925, cuando salió *La mužer onesta*, el judeo-español estaba comenzando su proceso de decadencia. Posiblemente el vocabulario de la novela hubiera sido más rico, menos afrancesado, si hubiera salido setenta años antes.

Las principales características de la novela en lengua sefardí son su dependencia sobre fuentes extranjeras y su forma serializada o de entregas. Olga Borovaya destaca que tal situación sucede cuando la literatura en cuestión es joven, débil y cuando la cultura se encuentra en un momento crucial de cambio[14]. Efectivamente, no cabe duda de que una importante proporción de narrativa judeo-española fue traducida de otras lenguas, como se ve por la cantidad de novelas que se anuncian como "tresladado", "rezumido", "imitado", "adaptado" o aranžado"[15]. La mayoría de estas obras eran francesas, entre ellas obras de Dumas, Hugo, Prevost, Sue, Zola, Verne y otras de menos transcendencia. Si de una parte es posible insistir que la traducción misma ofrece una vía al desarrollo de un estilo propio, de otra es posible que la profusión de traducciones ahogara la creatividad literaria[16].

Eliya Rafael Karmona

Eliya Karmona[17] nació en Constantinopla en 1869, muriendo allí en 1932. Descendía de una vieja familia respetada y acomodada, dedicada a la administración y la banca[18].

Karmona estudió con una *maestra* y luego en la escuela judía, la *Talmud Torah*, desde donde a la edad de once años pasó al colegio de la *Alliance,*donde, después de cuatro años se le colocó como profesor de francés de los hijos del Gran Vizir. A raíz de las graves pérdidas financieras sufridas por la familia Karmona, el padre de Eliya terminó como funcionario menor de tranvías. Eliya por su parte perdió su puesto y durante cierto tiempo trabajó vendiendo fósforos en la calle. Tuvo la suerte de colocarse como aprendiz en la imprenta de *El Tyempo*, importante periódico ladino. El sueldo era mísero, por lo cual Eliya abandonó la imprenta. Después de una juventud aventurera cuando se dedicó sin gran éxito a muchas profesiones, y sufrió a veces grave pobreza,volviendo a veces a *El Tyempo*, y viajando a

Salónica y Esmirna y hasta al Cairo, regresó otra vez al diario, quedando esta vez hasta 1908 como tipógrafo y a la vez escritor de novelas.

La carrera de Karmona como autor de narrativas había empezado en 1899, cuando él mismo imprimió *konšežikas* o cuentos dictados por su madre. Pasó a escribir novelas — su obra totaliza casi sesenta obras[19] – hasta que en 1902 la censura prohibió la edición de narrativas con temática de robos, asesinos y amor, Karmona se marchó a Egipto donde la censura era menos dura. Desafortunadamente no abundaban en Alejandría lectores de la clase de novela judeo-española que Karmona escribía, motivando su vuelta a Constantinopla y a *El Tyempo*.

Desde 1908, cuando la revolución de los "Jóvenes Turcos" libera la prensa y las editoriales de la fuerte censura anterior, Karmona dirige y redacta la mayor parte si no todo el periódico humorístico *El Ǧugeton*.

En palabras de Amelia Barquín, Karmona fue,

> [...] un tipo de intelectual sefardí frecuente en esta época, caracterizado por su hacer polifacético e inquieto, por su intensa actividad y su movilidad en las diferentes parcelas de la cultura, en contacto con los nuevos ideales de modernización...[...][20]

La Mužer Onesta

La novela o *romanso* ladino suele ser más bien corta. Tomando como ejemplos las novelas que se encuentran en la colección de la *British Library*[21], los ejemplos son de 14, 76, 16, 112, 45, 26, 56, 18, 32, 58, 68, 82, 52, 177, 60, 26, 40, 224, 15, 14, 64, 141, 523, 224, 191, 20, 18, y 53 páginas. La mayoría de aquellas novelas que tienen más de cien páginas son traducciones, principalmente del francés.

La mužer onesta, que no se anuncia como traducción ni adaptación, aunque la figura literaria de la mujer injustamente sospechada de infiel por su marido es corriente en la narrativa y el drama, tiene 111 páginas, de tamaño 16º, con un total de unos 16.000 palabras, es decir lo que en inglés se llama una *novelette*. Tiene 21 capítulos (en realidad 20, porque un número viene saltado entre 5 y 7) divididos entre 7 entregas de 16 páginas.[22] La última página (112) contiene publicidad para la próxima novela (*Demandar Todos El Romanso La Kunyada Sin Korason*). El editor como tal no existe. Podemos suponer que Karmona entregaba sus cuartillas directamente a la imprimería Suhalit, y luego pasaba las hojas a Benjamín B. (probablemente Behar) Joseph, conocido distribuidor de libros. La entrega normalmente valía un gruš, suma cuya equivalente debe comprenderse dentro de la escala de precios generales, pero se puede suponer, por la ausencia de láminas y de cubiertas, que era suficientemente económico para caber dentro del presupuesto de muchas familias.[23]

Tema de la Novela

Probablemente, un estudio profundizado de la obra total de Karmona produciría más ejemplos de la actitud demostrada por la heroína de *La mužer onesta*, cuando declara:

> [...]kuanto mas un ombre sela a su mužer, mas el la ovliga a azer lo negro. La onestidad deve venir de si, i no ordenada de su marido.

Lo importante es que Karmona juzgaba este tema como apropiado e interesante para inspirar una novela que él quería vender al público lector judío de Constantinopla, Salónica, Esmirna y Jerusalén de los años 20 del siglo pasado. No es importante remover fuentes para buscar si el adulterio y la seducción de mujeres casadas representaban una realidad corriente entre cierto sector próspero y muy afrancesado de la burguesía judía ladinoparlante de la época. En todo caso, como se verá, el autor no se preocupa por situar su novela en un lugar dado. Sí podemos decir que el adulterio y la seducción

107

sucedían tan frecuentemente en los romances cantados de los sefardíes que los que leían la novela o la escuchaban leer, no se hacían quizás tantas aspas ante el tema como se hubiera hecho en otra sociedad más gazmoña[24]. Podemos suponer que la novela de aventuras, tan típica en el corpus ladino, con sus bandidos, contrabandistas, asesinatos, vampirismo y cadáveres que hablan, ofrecía menos interés a las mujeres que una novela como *La mužer onesta*, o como *Anna María o el korazon de mužer* (1905), de Alejandro ben Ghiyyat, donde la esposa infértil adopta al niño ilegítimo de su marido infiel[25]. En todo caso, en 1925, fecha de la edición de *La mužer onesta*, Karmona, nacido en 1869, tenía 56 años, y ya no pertenecía a la generación de los personajes de la novela, aunque él tuvo sus aventuras románticas[26]. Sin embargo, el tema de la novela ha debido ser aceptable para sus lectores, o más bien lectoras, del mismo modo de que en épocas más tardes sus hijas leerían ávidamente el periodismo de "peluquería" que trata de la vida íntima de las estrellas del cine, de las mujeres de futbolistas y de personajillos pertenecientes a las familias reales. Es más; suponiendo que la lectura de esta novela, que no sabemos si se editó primero como folletín de periódico pero que nos ha llegado en forma de libro, tuviera lugar en la sala de estar, quizás los sábados por la tarde, podemos imaginar que alguien lo leyera en alta voz, y que las mujeres de la casa asentaban con movimientos de la cabeza cada vez que uno de los amigos de Armand afea su plan de que ellos traten de seducir a Žulyeta, y que se regocijaban cuando ella, sin bajar un ápice de su dignidad, consigue demostrar a su marido las consecuencias de sus celos, consecuencias que por el comportamiento *onesto* de ella, él logra evitar. En efecto, aunque la mujer es a menudo protagonista de la novela judeo-española, aquí Žulyeta no es ni la dominatriz, ni la seductora, ni el ángel víctima de la crueldad de los hombres, sino una mujer tranquila, con gran aplomo, y al final triunfadora sin triunfalismos. La "pyedad" para ella no significa, como lo entienden hombres como Armand, la debilidad. Ella es todo lo contrario de la perezosa consumidora de café y de cigarros, la mujer oriental degenerada pintada por los informes de la *Alliance*[27]. Žulyeta es afrancesada por su educación y su formación. Ha sido aculturada para no reaccionar con sorpresa a las declaraciones de amor que recibe de Maurice y los otros jóvenes. Protesta contra el intento de seducción pero no porque el adulterio ofenda valores religiosos. En esto refleja su secularización, la cual sin embargo no contradice su amor-propio como mujer y su lealtad como esposa. Žulyeta como personaje refleja la campaña de cincuenta años antes, cuando los periódicos instruccionales del siglo XIX, *El Sol*, *El amigo de la familya* y *El Instruktor,* se dirigían hacia la mujer como instrumento de cambio, mientras en su *La cortesiya o reglas del buen komportamyento* (Constantinopla 1871) Rosa Gabbai defendía la formación intelectual femenina[28].

Llama la atención el que no haya referencias algunas judías en la novela, salvo el que los personajes hablan ladino, que ostentan nombres europeos típicos del afrancesamiento de jóvenes sefardíes de la época, y que entre el vocabulario que emplean aparecen de vez en cuando las palabras *mazaloso* o *desmazalado*, palabras hebreas ("afortunado" y "desafortunado") que entraron en el español hablado de los judíos españoles. Sin embargo, David Fresko, director de *El Tyempo*, proclamó que si un judío leía acerca de cualquier tema escrito en una lengua empleada sólo por judíos, el texto retenía su carácter judío[29]. Aunque puede parecer esto una especie de paradoja, no lo es tanto si se piensa en la literatura como algo *recibido* por el lector. Sólo aquellos judíos que sabían el ladino, leían *La mužer onesta*.

En Comparacion Con El Yidico

Inevitablemente, el lector hace una comparación entre la producción literaria del español sefardí y la de las extensas regiones donde se hablaba el yídico, el alemán medieval que los judíos habían traído consigo al abandonar las zonas alemanófonos para el oriente eslavo.

Superficialmente, hay cierto parecido en la situación de ambas lenguas. Los judíos habían traído consigo una lengua de la Europa occidental, transmitiéndola por muchas generaciones a la vez que se encontraban rodeados de lenguas sin ningún parecido a la suya. Ahora bien, la comparación puede llevar en algunos casos a conclusiones falsas. En primer lugar, las demografías eran completamente diferentes. Frente a los varios millones de personas cuya lengua materna era el yídico, es dudoso que hubiera en su máxima extensión más de trescientas mil personas ladinoparlantes Quizás por esto mismo, sería difícil decir que la literatura laica novelística en ladino sea de alta calidad en comparación con la novela yídica de los siglos XIX y XX.

¿Se debe esto al deterioro intelectual del mundo sefardí reflejado en la comparativamente menor creación de literatura filosófica y de derecho judío [*halakhá*]. El choque experimentado en el siglo XVII por el falso mesías Šabetai Tsvi, junto con el temor a un resurgimiento del sabateísmo (los últimos seguidores de este movimiento, los *dönmeh*, siguen viviendo en Turquía), y la resolución rabínica de dominar los impulsos antinomianos, hicieron más estrechos los horizontes intelectuales[30]. Si se cree que la novela existe para describir y criticar la sociedad que la produce, la novela judeo-española era más bien inferior en comparación con el examen y crítica de la sociedad judía realizada por las grandes obras en lengua yídica. Aun la novela de Ben-Yitshak Saserdote *Rafael i Miryam* (1910) subtitulada *Novela de la vida de los Ǧudiyos de Oriente*, corresponde poco a su título[31]. Por otra parte, ¿cómo se explica la ausencia en la novela judeo-española de referencias judías y hebreas — a la liturgia, la Biblia y los textos rabínicos — aun los juegos de palabras —, tan frecuentes en la literatura yídica y hebrea contemporánea a la de los sefardíes? ¿Será porque los novelistas sefardíes no habían recibido la intensa formación talmúdica con la cual se criaron los novelistas yídicos tales como Shalom Rabinovitz (Sholem Aleijem, 1859-1916), Isaac Leib Peretz (1852-1915) y Shalom J. Abramovitz (Mendele Moyjer S'forim [1836-1917])? El sistema tradicional sefardí de pasar desde la *maestra* al *meldar* (escuela primera) y luego al *Talmud Torah* o nivel secundario, había perdido prestigio frente a la enseñanza que ofrecían los colegios de la *Alliance*. En efecto, la *Alliance* consiguió absorber los *Talmud Torah*. Aun así, dada la larga tradición de estudiar material religioso en lengua española, Biblia, Psalmos, Cantar de los Cantares, Proverbios, cantos para nacimientos, circuncisiones y bodas, sermones, *Hagadá, Coplas de Purim,* para no decir el *Me'am Lo'ez*, parece extraña la ausencia, por lo menos en *La mužer onesta,* de ritmos o fraseologías de origen religioso.

Muy probablemente hubo motivos lingüísticos que explican el atraso literario del español sefardí en comparación con el yídico. Este se encontraba rodeado de diversos idiomas europeos, algunos de los cuales poseían una tradición literaria rica. En contraste, no existía ningún contacto geográfico y muy poca relación cultural entre el yídico y el castellano peninsular. De modo que, cuando el autor ladino necesitaba nuevas palabras, e incluso cuando en realidad tales palabras ya existían, echaba mano al francés que había aprendido en el colegio de la *Alliance*. Así es como, por ejemplo, por *desear* se decía *suetar*, siguiendo el galicismo *souhaiter*.

En contraste, aun en la tan atrasada Rusia tsarista, las exigencias culturales del lector yídico eran en términos generales mayores que las del lector de ladino. Los grandes novelistas en yídico, multilingües y con profunda preparación en la cultura judía y la general, conociendo las obras de Gogol, Turgenev, Tolstoy y Dostoyevski, disfrutaban de un público donde no faltaban lectores 'ideales'. Es más, El riquísimo tejido de la vida judía política y cultural empleaba la lengua yídica en sus

111

actividades, de forma que al yídico se le fue aceptando como una lengua escrita tan apropiada como el aristocrático hebreo.

El ladino carecía de una tradición narrativa. Los modelos para Karmona y los otros novelistas sefardíes orientales eran los grandes autores extranjeros, principalmente franceses, cuya riqueza de lengua no sabían imitar los novelistas sefardíes. Se escribía periodismo y narrativa en un idioma que los autores juzgaban apropiado para gente poco culta — por antonomasia las mujeres — personas a quienes no se podía dirigir en la lengua de máximo estatus cultural, es decir, el francés. Eliya Karmona dio como su motivo por escribir en ladino el que "Avyendo remarkado ke el ke melda el espanyol, es akel ke no konose ni el turko ni el franses, yo empesi a eskrivir en un linguaže popular ke mesmo kriaturas i vyežas lo entendiyan."[32]. Igualmente, en 1908, en el primer número de su periódico humorístico *El Ǧugeton*, Karmona escribe

El Ǧugeton va ser eskrito en un linguaže mui fasil y mui koryente sigun azemos tambyen por nuestros romansos.

En esto Karmona no era innovador. Ya en 1871 Rosa Gabbai, hija de Yejezquel Gabbai, fundador de *El Telégrafo* y juez de los tribunales turcos, escribía en el prólogo a su libro *La cortesiya o reglas del buen komportamyento*:

syendo por la prima ves, mosotros mos dimos una pena fuerte de dešar atras las avlas espanyolas verdaderas porke no les seya enfastyo a las ke no las entyenden i buškimos de servirmos de lengua espanyola oryentala kon la esperansa ke esta nuestra ovra topara grasya ya en prezensyas de las senyoras i senyores i sera para mi y para otras komo mi un koražo por kontinuar en trezladar i ordenar livros por el adelantamyento de nuestra nasyon...

Es quizás lícito, por lo tanto, preguntarse si, suponiendo contrafactualmente un comienzo anterior de la real para la narrativa en lengua sefardí, el español de Oriente hubiera producido su Mendele o su Singer.

¿Como juzgar el valor de la novela judeo-espanola?

El contraste entre la mediocridad de la novela en ladino y la alta calidad a la que llega la literatura yídica, es tan grande que uno no puede menos de preguntarse si existe alguna utilidad en tratar de discutir críticamente la narrativa judeo-española. Es difícil aplicar criterios modernos a las obras sobrevivientes de las 254 novelas que cita Altabé en su repertorio o las más de 500 que calcula Romero[33]. En primer lugar muchas ya no existen físicamente o se guardan en un solo ejemplar en una biblioteca. Sólo unas pocas han sido presentadas en ediciones modernas.

Ahora bien, podemos empezar preguntándonos, para aplicar algunos de los criterios de la crítica literaria, si las novelas sefardíes son fantasías y pasatiempos para momentos libres, o si reflejan el mundo real. Los lectores de *La mužer onesta* ¿conseguían identificarse con Armand, Žulyeta y los otros, con sus emociones, temores, y rencores? Las novelas ¿permiten el empleo del juicio moral? ¿Le ofrecen al lector un desafío a sus supuestos?

Contestando estas preguntas, la verdad es que aprendemos poco de las relaciones humanas, el amor, los celos, el sacrificio, las aspiraciones o las transigencias. La novela judeo-española no se presta a un análisis sofisticado. Son los adjetivos y adverbios, una construcción elaborada de tiempos y modos de verbos, más un gran acervo de léxico los elementos que le permiten al novelista profundizar en las emociones y pensamientos de sus personajes. Estas herramientas parecen faltar en la novela sefardí, la cual no posee la riqueza de léxico que al autor le permitiera seleccionar la palabra justa. En general, ni el argumento, ni los personajes ni el diálogo mueven al lector acostumbrado a la gran novela europea.

La mužer onesta carece del monólogo interior, sea que lo presente el personaje o el narrador omnisciente, donde el protagonista comunique sus reacciones, discuta interiormente lo que piensa de su interlocutor, penetre en sus propios motivos y los de los otros. Para hacer todo esto, la lengua debe tener la potencia de expresar todos los detalles menudos de la realidad exterior e interior. *El Tyempo* publicó en 1893 un serie de artículos insistiendo que al ladino le faltaban un léxico para expresar sentimiento e ideas[34].Por esto, los escritores no tenían más remedio que echar mano al léxico francés. Parece, no obstante, que el ladino hubiera podido, por lo menos en teoría, *españolizar* el vocabulario de la literatura francesa que sus escritores sabían leer. La cuestión es si los lectores hubieran comprendido las meditaciones, análisis, generalizaciones y evaluaciones morales, y las herramientas conceptuales y las modulaciones de tono exigidas.

La técnica de la novela en judeo-español tampoco es muy refinada. No existe en la novela análisis del pensamiento individual. Casi no hay soliloquios. Las opiniones de cada cual se expresan por medio de conversaciones breves en un léxico limitado. Las expresiones se repiten de manera cursi- '"*le hižo un calurozo resibo*' o '*Madame, me muero por vos*'" — hasta el punto que a menudo el lector puede terminar la frase casi sin leerla.

La construcción de *La mužer onesta* es escueta. Se trata de una obra con seis personajes, los cuales se interrelacionan ficcionalmente durante unos diez o doce días, sin que haya ni largos viajes ni grandes intervalos de tiempo. No hay más de un tema. En realidad, la novela tiene las características de una pieza de teatro con unos cuantos lugares de actuación (casa y patio de Armand y Žulyeta, oficina de Armand, calle, hotel donde vive Rišard, teatro). ¿Es posible que la novela tenga su origen en una comedia, quizás del autor armenio Minokian Mardaros cuyo teatro confiesa Karmona que plagió? Karmona editó otra novela, *El marido zeloso*, con tema semejante, en el Cairo en 1907, reeditado en 1922-1923[35]

Es quizás importante examinar la relación entre la literatura y la sociedad, irrespectivamente del mérito literario de las obras en cuestión.Quizás deberíamos considerar la novela judeo-española un poco como pensamos en el cine en sus primeras décadas. La obra cinemática se desplegaba ante un público poco sofisticado, que exigía una línea narrativa bien definida, con una descripción breve pero muy acentuada, sin reflexiones monológicas por parte del autor/narrador, y que respondiera a sus propios prejuicios y supuestos. El público que leía o ante quien se leía en alta voz la novela judeo-española había visto el ladino escrito sólo en textos litúrgicos o en el *Me'am Lo'ez*. Muchos, sobre todo las mujeres, nunca habían leído su propia lengua. Y por supuesto, pocos habían leído una novela en otra lengua o a lo más algunos extractos de una novela francesa o una poesía de La Fontaine. Admitamos que tenemos delante un género de "infraliteratura" que corresponde a los siguientes modelos:

1. El autor se intromete (Karmona dice a veces "loke nuestros lektores ya konosen")

2. El autor manipula inverosimilmente la narrativa, incluso con incompetencia técnica, por ejemplo en la revelación de parte de Žulyeta de que tuvo unas "aventuras" antes de casarse, cuando el autor ya ha presentado a Žulyeta al lector como hija de familia de gran honor.

3. Simplifica exageradamente.

4. Busca reflejar una conciencia colectiva en la forma de una filosofía simplificada.

5. No se preocupa por cuestiones sociales ni políticas.

La finalidad de las novelas judeo-españolas era divertir a los lectores y vender los periódicos en los cuales tales novelas aparecían. Leer una narrativa ficcional constituía una gran novedad, como visitar el cine lo era también. Ahora bien, pese a que *La mužer onesta* no se anuncia como una narrativa de judíos de Constantinopla, es evidente que se proponía decir algo de un mundo que no se encontraba muy lejos del de los lectores: el mundo judío y el contexto de matrimonio, amores y celos.

No hay que olvidar las condiciones de producción. Aun en esta novela de 111 páginas, la prisa general de la narración, la poca extensión de los fascículos o entregas, y la necesidad de frecuentes momentos dramáticos, reflejan las condiciones de escribir que sufrían los autores, los cuales también a menudo redactaban gran parte de los periódicos en los cuales las novelas salían. Se escribía contra reloj, sin poder corregir el trabajo. Había que entregar sin falta cierto número de cuartillas con un léxico limitado.

La novela en español sefardí refleja, con todo, la vida y la cultura de un mundo hispanohablante que tristemente ya casi no existe.

Ediciones contemporáneas de novelas judeo-españolas

Amelia Barquín, "Doce novelas judío-españolas" (1995, véase nota 9)

L. Carracedo, *El rey y el šastre* (*Estudios Sefardíes*, 1 1978, págs. 399-410)

M. del Rosario Martínez González, *Historia interesante de el emperador Basil el segundo y el rabí*, bajo el título *Un marido entre dos mujeres* (Barcelona: Ameller, 1978). También hay traducción al inglés por Sita Sheer: *The Rabbi had Two Wives* (Jerusalén 1985).

R. Loewenthal, Autobiografía de Eliya Karmona (1984 véase nota 17).

Gaëlle Collin: Edition d'une nouvelle judéo-espagnole. *El ombre de la pendola* de Viktor Leví, (*Neue Romania 22*) 1999, págs. 51-70),

Gaëlle Collin, E. Karmona *La novya aguna. (Neue Romania 26, 2002)*

Pilar Romeu, transliteración de Alejando Pérez, *Syempre Ǧudiya*, (Granada: *Miscelánea de Estudios Arabes y Hebraicos*), Sección de hebreo Vol.46, 1997, págs. 117-135.

Sandra Bennett (Universidad de Londres, 2005) "Neglected Heritage of the Jews of the Ottoman Empire from 1885 to 1922", incluye transcripciones de *Anna Maria*, de Alexandro Benghiat y de la traducción de la novela romántica francesa *Paul et Virginie.*

1   Nos basamos en la obra de Elena Romero, *La creación literaria en lengua sefardí*, Madrid, Mapfre, 1992.

2   Ver A. Ben-Ur, "Ladino in Print: Towards a Comprehensive Bibliography", *Jewish History*, 16 (No.3) 2002, 309-326.

3   Ver Lehmann, M, "The Intended Reader of Ladino Rabbinic Literature and Judeo-Spanish Reading Culture", *Jewish History* 16, No. 3 (2002), 283-307.

4   Romero, 93. No hemos podido representar todas las señales diacríticas que esta especialista emplea.

5   Lehman, artículo citado.

6   Ver M.D. Gaón, *Ha-Itonut be-ladino*: *bibliografiyya,* Jerusalén, Instituto Ben-Zvi, 1965.

7   El tratado de Berlín de 1878 concedió la independencia a Bulgaria, Serbia, Rumanía y Montenegro, mientras el Tratado de Londres de 1913 le dejó al imperio sólo un mínimo de territorio en Europa.

8   Ver Rodrigue, A, *French Jews, Turkish Jews: the Alliance Israélite Universelle and the Politics of Jewish Schooling in Turkey 1860-1925*, Bloomington, Indiana University Press, 1990, y Benbassa, E., "L'Education féminine en Orient; l'école des filles de l'Alliance Israélite Universelle à Galata, Istanbul (1879-1912)", *Histoire, Economie et Société*, 4 (1991), 529-559. Agradezco a Mlle. Gaëlle Collin el haberme enviado una copia de este artículo.

9   Amelia Barquín, *Edición y estudio de doce novelas aljamiadas sefardíes de principios del siglo XX*, tesis de doctorado editado por Servicio Editorial de la Universidad del País Vasco, Vitoria, 1997, 77.

10   "No nos preocupamos de la masa semi-analfabeta hasta que las escuelas hayan abierto una brecha en la muralla de la que se fortifica el fanatismo".Citado por Strauss, J, "Who read what in the Ottoman Empire (19th and 20th centuries)?", *Middle Eastern Literatures*, 6, 1, enero de 2003, 39-76. Ver en contraste, Bennett, S, "Neglected Heritage: the Secular Literature of the Jews of the Ottoman Empire from 1885 to 1922" tesis de Queen Mary University of London, 2004, 38, quien hace la pregunta oportuna de si el fenómeno de productividad literaria hubiera acontecido aun sin el estímulo de la *Alliance*.

11   Como ejemplos, el semanal hebreo *Hayom*, de San Petersburgo (1890-1) imprimía diez mil ejemplares; su sucesor era *Hatsefira* de Varsovia; *Hashiloah y Hamelitz* salían de Odesa, mientras tres diarios hebreos circulaban en Varsovia (ver Sarah A. Stein, *Making Jews Modern: the Yiddish and Ladino Press in the Russian and Ottoman Empires,*

Bloomington: Indiana University Press, 2004, 27, 48, 49).

[12] Henri Nahum, *Juifs de Smyrne, XIXe-XXe siècles*, París, Aubier, 1977, 102, citando informes de la *Alliance*.

[13] Véase M. Alpert, "Dr. Angel Pulido and Philo-Sephardism in Spain", *Jewish Historical Studies*, 40, 2005, 105-119. Ver el estudio preliminar de María Antonia Bel Bravo a la obra principal de Pulido, *Españoles sin patria y la raza sefardí* (republished, Granada, 1993).

[14] Ver Olga Borovaya, "The Serialized Novel as Rewriting: the Case of Ladino Belles-Lettres", *Jewish Social Studies*, 10, 1, 1993, 30-68.

[15] Ver David Altabé, "The Romanzo 1900-1933; a Bibliographical Survey", *The Sephardic Scholar*, III, 96-109, 1977-1978. Este estudio se basa en Avraham Ya'ari, *Catalogue of Judeo-Spanish Books in the Jewish National and University Library* (de Jerusalén), 1934.

[16] M. del Rosario Martínez González, *Historia interesante de el emperador Basil el segundo y el rabí*, bajo el título *Un marido entre dos mujeres* (Barcelona: Ameller, 1978), calcula a base de diversos catálogos un total de 303 novelas de las que cree que unas 130 son originales, la mayoría de ellas anónimas.

[17] Para la biografía de Karmona hemos empleado como fuentes Robyn K. Loewenthal, *Elia Karmona's Autobiography: Judeo-Spanish Popular Press and Novel Publishing Milieu in Constantinople, Ottoman Empire, circa 1860-1932*, 2 tomos, tesis doctoral, Universidad de Nebraska, Lincoln, 1984, y M-C. Varol, "L'Empire ottoman à travers la biographie picaresque d'Eliya Karmona", conferencia mecanografiada. La autobiografía en es asequible también en las páginas 479 y sigs. de la compilación de Rifat Birmizrahi, *Lo que meldavan nuestros padres* (Istanbul: Gözlem Gazeticilik Basin Ve Yayin 2006), edición en judeo-español, turco e inglés.

[18] Ver arbol genealógico en Loewenthal, p.20.

[19] Loewenthal págs. 578-609.

[20] Amelia Barquín, tesis cit., 87.

[21] Ver Ilana Tahan, "Sephardic and Judeo-Spanish Material in the British Library's Hebrew Collection", *Proceedings of the Thirteenth British Conference on Judeo-Spanish Studies (7-9 September 2003)*, coord. Hilary Pomeroy, Department of Hispanic Studies, Queen Mary, University of London, 2006, 177-240.

[22] El fenómeno del capítulo que salta un número también se nota en *La Novya aguna*, otra novela de Karmona.

[23] Comparar J. I. Ferreras, *La novela por entregas 1840-1950* (Madrid, 1972). El panorama en España no debe de haber

sido muy diferente del del mundo ladinófono.

24 Esther Benbassa "L'Education féminine..." cit.

25 Bennett, 136.

26 Varol, texto mecanografiado cit, 7.

27 Rodrigue 78.

28 Para *El Instruktor* ver Stein, cit, 127.

29 Stein, 125.

30 Es lo que sugiere Ya'akov Barnai en Goldberg. H. (comp.) *Sephardi and Middle East Jewries: History and Culture in the Modern Era,* Bloomington, Indiana University Press, 1996, 73-80, esp.75 y 79. Ver también Benbassa, E. y Rodrigue, A, *Sephardi Jewry: a History of the Judeo-Spanish Community, 14th-20th Centuries,* Berkeley, University of California Press, 2000, 60.

31 Ver David Altabé, "Parallels in the Development of Modern Turkish and Judeo-Spanish Literature", *Studies on Turkish-Jewish History,* Nueva York, Sepher-Hermon Press, 1996, 56-72.

32 Loewenthal, cit. Birmizrahi cit, 508.

33 Romero, 221.

34 Stein, 73.

35 Loewenthal, 588 y 601.

La Mužer Onesta
Provada Por Su Marido

Eliya R(afael). Karmona
Direktor Del Ǧugeton

(Constantinopla: Imprimeriya "Suholit")
5685*

Benjamin B (ehar). Joseph,
Libraire, Stamboul Barnathan Han Constantinople

---

*El año hebreo cambia en septiembre-octubre, de modo que
5685 puede significar 1924 o 1925

Nota Sobre La Transliteración

Hemos transliterado esta novela al alfabeto romano desde el tipo hebreo rabínico o *raší* en el cual fue imprimida. Algunos fonemas en castellano medieval no podían ser reproducidos en la ortografía hebrea sin el empleo de diacríticas. Para reproducir aquellos sonidos y con el fin de indicar cómo se pronuncian en el español sefardí de Oriente los hemos ortografiado de la forma siguiente:

A. Las letras hebreas *šin* y *zayin* encabezadas por una diacrítica, las cuales significan un sonido reflejado, por ejemplo, en la ortografía francesa por "ch" (*chapeau*) y "j" (*janvier*), o en inglés por "sh" (*shape*) y el grupo "su" sonora (*pleasure*), son ortografiados aquí š y ž.

B. La letra hebrea *gimmel* con diacrítica, que significa los dos fonemas *ch* y *dj* es ortografiada aquí *ch* (*muncho*) o dejada en ǧ (*ǧente* o *ǧudiyo*).

C. Para la combinación de *lamed* + *yod* + *yod*, hemos escrito *y* (*eya, yo* y *ya*).

D. En una palabra como ḥarvar, la *ḥ* con acento significa el sonido de la jota en castellano.

E. Hemos dejado la *d* intervocálica, señalada por una *dalet* con diacrítica, como *d*, mientras reproducimos la *bet* con diacrítica por la *v*.

F. En el caso de palabras que contienen el diptongo *ue*, tales como *nuestro* o *puedo*, aunque algunos especialistas lo transliteran como *we* (*nwestro*), esto nos ha parecido innecesario, excepto en el caso de *gue* (*vergwensa, gwerko*) donde en castellano moderno se escribe una diáresis encima de la u para indicar que se pronuncie la *u*.

G Hemos respetado las colocaciones tales como "ala" "dela" etc, cuyas palabras se imprimen juntas en el original.

Kapitulo 1

Era una manyanada de lunes, Armand Fredol i Žulyeta Gaskarin, rezen kazadikos, de 15 dyas, eran asentados uno enfrente de otro konversando las dulses avlas de la luna de myel. Žulyeta era muy gustoza y reiya kon su novyo en dizyendole:

"Grasyas al Dyo, despues de tres anyos de amor sinsero, el Dyo kižo byen aunar nuestros korasones."

Armand sonreiya a estas palavras i echava una mirada de akeas ke azen remenear el korason, en dežando a su novya kontinuar ansi:

"Dime te rogo, Armand, de mi ermozura te enamorates?"

"Byen siguro, si no eras ermoza, yo no te uvyere nunka tomado."

"I mi grasya? No tengo yo muncha grasya?"

"Muncha, mi kerida, devo felisitarme de aver eskožido una mužer kon tanta grasya."

"I mi instruksyon?"

"Esto tambyen no te deša nada a desear. Solamente, si no te aravyas, Žulyet, te vo dezir una koza."

"Avla, kerido Armand, tengo alguna kulpa? Yo me korižire en vista[1]."

"No tyenes ninguna kulpa, mi kerida, ma...ay koza ke syempre ke la veo en ti, me bate el korason."

"Armand! Te rogo esplikarte mas presto, kero saver mi yerro i korežirme. Kualo tengo yo de feo?"

"No tyenes nada de feo, mi kerida, ma remarko munchas vezes ke kuando vyene algun musafir[2] le mostras muncha kara, I esto me esta displazyendo, la verdad ke te diga."

"Esto es el uzo del saver bivir."

"Si es sin apretarle la mano i sin sonreirte, no es, mužer?"

"La kortesiya egziže de azer un kalurozo resivo a todo

ken vyene a vižitar, ke sea ombre o mužer, no kreo ke se apega nada, en tokando a un la mano."

"Ma esto me aze pena, mi kerida, yo me selo, vergwensa es?"

"Te selas? Si te selas, es una prova ke no me keres byen."

"Ǧustamente la contra, kerida Žulyet, kuando un marido ama a su mužer, el deve selarse."

"Bavažadas[3]! Ni un ombre puede selar a su mužer, ni eya a su marido, es una lokura. Si de parte a parte ay una sinsera amistad[4], ninguno se enganyan de parte a parte."

"Tyenes muncha razon, mi kerida, ma, ay un punto prinsipal ke son pokos los ke lo konosen."

"En kinze dyas de kasado, empesar a selar, ke vergwensa!"

"No te aravyes, mi kerida, las mužeres no soš negras[5], ma soš muy pyadosas, I kuando un ombre ve ke en vinyendo a vižitar la amostras muncha ǧelvi[6], el profita de la okasyon de vuestra pyedad, por deklararvos el amor, dezirvos ke se esta muryendo por vos, lyorar munchas vezes a vuestros pyes, i vosotras ke tenes un korason blando, vos aǧiǧaš[7] de el i le azeš pyedad."

"Te olvidates, parese, ke las mužeres nasimos kon el gwerko[8] enǧuntos? Nunka una mužer enganya su marido si eya esta contente de el. Si veras algunas mužeres ke enganyan sus marido[9], deve aver algun buto[10]. O ke el marido no es a su grado, o ke el la enganya antes de eya, o ke la vida ke el marido le da a su mužer no es conforme a su manera de saver bivir. Ma mozotros ke esto sigura ke mos amamos de puro korason, ke tu soš un marido model, sigun ya te konosko, ke la instruksyon de ti i mi son las mezmas, I ke sos un marido ke no me dešas nada a dezear, por kualo tu mužer ke te enganye? No, Armand, no, no te seles, porke si te selas, sufres en la vida!... Ningun ombre puede selar a su mužer, ni su mužer a su marido, es una vanidad, sin pri[n]sipio y sin cavo, ke no trae otro profito ke el desrepozo en la vida."

"Esto puede ser, ma ke ke aga? Yo me selo! Y es la

muncha amistad ke tengo por ti, ke me ovliga a azerlo."

Žulyeta sonreiya a esta repuesta. Eya apanyava la mano de su marido, la pasaba por sus ožos i le deziya:

"No te seles, Armand, no te seles, ya tuvites *mazal*[11] de kaer en una mužer onesta."

"Esto lo se, i no tengo ninguna sope[12], ma es la natura ke me puša[13] a azerlo."

"Alora, no tyenes menester de traer ningun musafir en kaza ni ir mosotros a vižitar a ningun lugar. Kale[14] bivir una vida asolada," respondiya Žulyeta kon un tono un poko ravyozo.

Mirando ke su mužer se iva aravyar, Armand troko de tono i abrasando a su mužer, el le apego un bezo kerenyozo en disyendole:

"No te aravyes, mi kerida, no me va (*sic*) selar, estas contente?"

"Siguro, selar ke kere dezir? Azas (*sic*) vergwensa! Selar kere dezir, no tener konfiansa en la mužer. I esta deskonfiansa no deve tener nunka un marido si no prova a su mužer. Ya me provates y vites ke no so fiela?"

Esta repuesta aziyan (*sic)* tresalir de alegriya a nuestro žoven Armand. Su mužer le ordenava de provarla! I esto era una buena arma para konvenserse si el era enganyado.

El konversa kon su mužer otra medya ora, en trokando la konversasyon. Se viste, se saluda kon su kerida y va a su echo[15].

Kapitulo 2

Kuando Armand saliya a la kalye el no teniya mas akea mesma alegriya ke teniya en kaza antes medya ora. La observasyon ke su mužer le aviya echo sovre el selo le tokava el korason. I el biervo p r o v a r[16] ke Žulyeta le aviya dicho, lo azien[17] mas muncho pensar. El amava muncho a su mužer, i por consigwensa, no era feo si se selava, ma visto ke este[18] solo displaziya a su mužer, el se veiya ovligado a ovedeser en konformandose al sigundo dezeo de provarla si eya era onesta i si el ḥatišinazlik[19] ke eya aziya a los musafires era por dover de korteziya o por azerse atirar la amistad de alguno.

Le kedava agora una koza a pensar. Komo provar a su mužer? Kon ken deskuvrirse ke el keriya provar a su novia? Puedriya el entrar en este ğogo un poco eskandalozo?

Este penseryo no lo dešava reposado i el se iva a su magazin[20] triste i abatido.

El kapo impyegado lo resiviya kon enkanto[21].

"Ke vos akontesyo, Sr.[22] Armand? De ke estaš tan triste?"

"No tengo nada," respondyo Armand, "va te rogo envista lyamame a Sr. Maurice Flus[23], el ižo de mi asosiado, tengo menester de avlar kon el por un echo importante."

Sinko puntos[24] despues, Maurice ya era serka de Armand.

"Ah! Ya vinites?!* Esklamó Armand, — Bravo! Vamos enğuntos, tengo menester de avlarte de un echo importante."

Armand, tomando el braso a Maurice, saliyan del magazin i se ivan asentarsen en una braseriya.

Armand comandava dos biras.

---

*sic con punto de interrogación y de exclamación.

"Tan demanyana vamos a bevir bira? demando Maurice."

"No importa. Tengo a deskuvrirte un sekreto ke es solo tu ke lo deves saves [r].[25]"

"La verdad dezirte Armand, me estas metyendo en kuydado."

"No ay nada de kuydar, solamente kero ke me des un konsežo."

"Yo te vo konsežar a ti? Tu sos mas grande ke mi."

"Ya se, ma en vežes los chikos saven mas muncho delos[26] grandes."

"Avla, veremos."

"Ya saves komo tu i yo somos dos sinseros amigos ke nos frekuentamos del tyempo ke salimos dela eskola i ke de parte a parte nos konosimos munchos sekretos."

"Esto no ay duda."

"Ya me konoses tambyen ke myentras munchos anyos, yo ize muncha *ğaailik*[27] i ke koli[28] alas mužeres komo kolar una limonada."

"Esto tambyen ya lo se."

"I byen, konosyendo el karacter blando de las mužeres, yo me esto selando de mi mužer. Eya afito muy esvelta, muy simpatika, savyendo muy muncho bivir, eya aze un kaluroso resevu[29] a todo ken vyene a kaza a vižitar."

"Eya no aze ke[30] su dever."

"Ya es verdad, ma...a mi no me esta plazyendo. Ya saves enel mundo ke estamos a un ombre ke vyene a vižitar en kaza no syerve mostrarle muncha kayentur[31], el se va a otros pensyeros, i algun dya... ken save!... No se kualo ke diga."

"Tyenes razon, sitas[32] ladron sospechador. Estas kreendo todos los ombres komo ti[33]? Ke kuando enkontravas alguna mužer, antes algunos anyos, apenas la veyas, ya bužkavas a sombairla[34]? Todas las mužeres no son igual[35]. Tanto mas que estuvites azyendo tres anyos de amor i tu propyo me dišites ke por la primera ves, pudites enkontrar una mužer onesta."

"Esto es verdad, ma... komo ke te diga."

"Ainda ay kinze dyas ke kazates, ya es ora de selar?"

"Ǧustamente[36], oy demanyana en tomando el kafe, nuestra konversasyon entre mi i Žulyeta kayo sovre mi forma de selar. Eya tuvo grande desplazir kuando le diše ke me selo. I por toda repuesta eya me dišo: 'No me puedes selar si no me provas.'"

"Tu keres provarla?"

"Ǧustamente."

"Grande lokura."

"Lokura? De ke?"

"Siguro, kerer meter un *kyevrit*[37] al borde de la lumbre por provar si se asyende[38]. Byen siguro ke se va asender!"

"No es la mesma koza. Una mužer no se asyende de amor de un mansevo komo se asyende un kyevrit dela lumbre."

"Aze komo keres, yo no esto de akordo."

"Puede ser ke tu idea kon la mya seriya diferente. Solamente kero ke me agas un plazir."

"Sovre este echo?"

"Si!"

"Ke puedo yo azer?"

"Kero ke tu propyo buškes a provar a mi mužer."

"Yo ke la prove? Ke manera?"

"En deklarandole el amor?"

"Ke koza? Yo, ižo del asosyado vuestro ke deklare el amor a vuestra mužer?"

"Ǧustamente, ayi esta el prinsipal punto. Si mi mužer esta auzada[39] a trokar[40] amor, apunto va atorgar vuestra proposisyon, ma si eya es onesta, en vista ke le areš la deklarasyon, vos va ronǧar[41] i me lo va dezir i a mi tambyen."

"Veramente dezirvos, no keriya entrar yo en un echo semežante."

"Algun danyo tyenes? Agora mesmo vas a ir a mi kaza kon preteksto de dezir a mi mužer ke no me espere a komer porke vo ir ande un amigo a pransar[42]. Profitando de mi avsensya, te vas asentar un poko en kaza, vas a entrar en konversasyon kon eya y le vas a deklarar el amor. Si te aksepto[43], mos va salir pyanko[44] a ti i a mi. Si no, le vas a rogar ke no lo kite de la boka[45], y si guadro el sekreto tuyo y no me dišo nada a mi, es ke eya guadra de mi todos sus sekretos i ke ya tyenes esperansa de reušir[46]. Yo te vo mandar despues una sigunda i una tersera ves, i ansi vo provar la onestidad de mi mužer."

"Kale[47] ke seya ke vos biveš muy alegre en vuestra kaza i kereš trokar la alegriya en tristeza."

"Yo devo estar siguro de loke tengo en mano."

Sr. Maurice se metyo a pensar i el respondyo enfin:

"Por azervos plazir yo vo ir, ma no estaš azyendo una buena idea."

"Tu va, el resto es mi echo."

Nuestro žoven Maurice Flus posava apunto su chapeo[48] en la kaveza i se iva a vižitar ala kaza ke konosemos.

Kapitulo 3

Del primer momento ke Armand saliya de kaza la ora de la konversasyon ke nuestros lektores ya vyeron, Žulyeta kedava ayi triste i abatida, y sin kererlo, un afrito[49] de korason la aziya yorar.

"Desdichada de mi, esklamava eya, ke ke azer teniya yo, una iža de prove, kazarme kon este riko? Muncha moneda! Poka vida!"

Entrega 2*

"Ainda ay kinze diyas ke kazimos, ya se esta selando, y el Dyo lo save si mas tadre, el no me va defender[50] de salir mesmo ala kaye."

Selar!... Ke koza es selar! Si yo so negra, sinkuenta selos de mi marido no valen un soldo, loko ke es este, kuanto mas un ombre sela a su mužer, mas el la ovliga a azer lo negro. La onestidad deve venir de si, i no ordenada de su marido.

Eya avlaba ansi, kuando subito la mosa vino informarla ke sinyor Maurice Fluš, el ižo del asosyado de su marido, veniya y dezeava verla.

"Azeldo entrar al salon," dižo.

I Žulyeta se diriğiya de parte del salon, esperando enpies el aribo de su auspido[51].

Kuando Maurice entro ala kamareta Žulyeta empeso a kaminar serka de el por resibirlo en dizyendole:

"Seas byen venido, Sr. Maurice, vuestra vižita entre el diya, en un diya entre la semana, me aze muncho enkantar[52]."

"No tengaš nada a pensar, Madame[53]. Vuestro marido vyendome ke iva pasar por aki, me enkargo de venir

---

*fascículo o episodio vendido cada semana.

130

dezirvos ke no va venir a komer al medyo diya porke esta invitado a komer en otro lugar."

"Vos ringrasyo[54], Sr. Maurice, i vos rogo de egskuzar el deranžo ke vos kavsa esta misyon de mi marido."

"Ah! Del todo[55], Madame, al kontraryo, esta misyon me izo enchir de alegriya, porke la verdad dezirvos, teniya eskarinyo[56] de vervos. I yo kontenti mi deseyo en vinyendo aki.."

"Teniyas eskarinyo de verme?" Esklamo Žulyet, "Kuryoso. Lo mas de las noches estaš aki, i ke ay de eskarinyar?"

"Ya es verdad, ma[57]... Madame, no saveš loke yo se. Ĝustamente indagora, avlando kon vuestro marido, le diše ke es el mas venturoso del mundo en tenyendo una mužer komo vos, i fue mesmo esta dezirle ke no konose la valor, sigun yo vos apresio!"

"I a mi marido, no se le volto la kolor de kara?"

"Un poko."

"El es muy seloso, sin saver ke tyene una mužer onesta."

"Todas las mužeres son onestas ma... Madame... en vezes crese en la güerta loke no kere el gwertelano. Sin kererlo, una mužer se puede ḥarvar[58] de amor de un ombre, komo sin kererlo, yo me ḥarvi de amor por vos, amor ke mezu[59] dezir indagora el eskarinyo ke teniya por vervos."

Esta fraze aziya demodar la kolor de kara de Madame Žulyet, ke respondiya kon muncho kalmo.

"Batalyateš una puerta muy yerada, Sr. Maurice, no so yo de akeas mužeres aristokratas ke por azer sus plazeres o sus lusos, ḥarvan la puerta del korason delos otros. No, Sr., yo, la ižika de un prove, onde la kapital de mi padre era la onestidad, i es dentro este kapital ke yo me engrandesi."

"Ma, Madame, no teneš un poko de pyedad por mi. Las mužeres fueron syempre muy pyadosas."

"Es verdad, para dar la limosna."

"Alora, Madame, no vo tener la ventura de resibir de

vuestra parte una repuesta favoravle?"

"Nunka! Anke mi marido es seloso i ke un seloso merece ke lo enganyen, yo no le are nunka esta traisyon."

"Ma Madame, me esto muryendo por vos. Sin vos, la vida es muy amarga."

"Echalde un poko de asukar ke se adulse. No puedo nunka azer traisyon a mi marido!"

"Alora, devo pedrer toda esperansa?"

"Byen siguro, Sr. Maurize, buškad a batalyar otra puerta."

Maurice se levantava por saludar i Žulyet no le dava la mano en dizyendole:

"Andad en buena ora, Sr. Maurice, no vos merekiyes[60], ni tengaš la vida amarga, en plasa ay munchas mužeres ke pueden muy byen adulsar vuestra vida."

Maurice se retirava i Žulyeta kedava sola, deziya entre si:

"Indagora ainda avlimos kon mi marido del selo, i medya ora despues este sinyor ke se dize ser amigo de mi marido, me deklara el amor. Un amor krudo ke se ve et[61] pošado[62] por alguno."

Eya se metiyo un poko un poko a pensar, i kontinuo en esklamando:

"Ya topi! Es el gwerko ke me va enganyar i mas ninguno. Oy demanyana, kuando avlimos kon mi marido, yo le diše ke me prove antes ke me sele! Por muy siguro, el mando a Maurice para ke me prove! Esto es, i otra koza no!... Tanto mižor, la repuesta de Maurice le ara ver una ves de mas, mi onestidad."

"Atavanado[63] de marido, el lo[64] save ke kuando una mužer kere azer una negrigura, ni provas azen ayre, ni senyales, ni maraviyas. Eya que save topar su tyempo, sin ke del todo se syenta. Torpe de marido!... El no esta puedyendo konoser mi valor."

Kapitulo 4

Nuestro seloso Armand esperava kon dispasensya el aribo de Maurice.

"Son muy raras las mužeres onestas", deziya el, "i esto siguro ke Maurice va reušir."

Myentras dos oras y medya el era enpyes en su kamareta de eskritoryo, dando bueltas de ariba abašo, i enchendo y vazyendo sigaros.

Subito, sus ožos se aklararon. Maurice veniya de entrar[65] a su kamareta.

"Ke eres, Maurice? Salyo loke diše yo?"

"Muy dura te la kreo el Dyo, tyenes grande šans[66] de tener una mužer onesta."

"En tan presto ya la konosites?"

"Bah! No se tyene menester muncho tyempo para konoser. Las palavras ke yo le avli i las rogativas ke yo le ize, si su korason era de fyerro[67] kaliya ke se ablandara."

"Es posivle ke fue por la primera ves ke se komporto ansi, si tu kontinuas a ir regularmente a mi kaza puede ser eya te atorgara."

"Ma eya me ronǧo de kaza, mon šer[68], porke tuve el koraže de apretarle un poko mas la mano."

"Alora, krees tu ke mi mužer es onesta?"

"Byen siguro, mas de onesta."

"Kon una prova, no me puedo konvenser! Devo azer una sigunda. Manyana mesmo yo buškare un otro porke la prove."

"Se ve komo sos bovo, por no yamarte torpe! Esta mužer ke va ver ke oy fui yo a deklararle el amor i ke manyana va ir un otro, eya se va akodrar mui presto loke te dišo ke la proves, i va entender ke la estas provando."

"I ke ke aga?"

"Al menos deves esperar un mes, i despues mandar un otro."

"Esta idea es buena, Tyenes razon. Yo esperare un mes,

portanto[69]."

"Solamente, una koza no estas pensando ke deviyas pensar antes de desidarte a mandar un inspektor para egzaminar el k o r a s o n[70] de tu mužer."

"La kuala?"

"Tu propyo puedes provar agora si tu mužer es onesta, sin ke tengas menester de ninguno."

"Ke manera la puedo provar?"

"Se ve ke el selo te esta topando la konsensya."

"No esto entendyendo kualo me keres dezir."

"Yo te kero dezir ke, si ala noche kuando te vas a kaza tu mužer no te avla nada de loke le paso oy, es ke ya estava kontente de mi proposisiyon y puede ser ay esperanza. Ma si eya te resive kon kara bruta, te konta la istoria i avla mal de mi, esto sinyifika ke su refuzo verso mi, es seryoso, i ke eya es onesta."

"I esta idea es buena! Yo no vo esperar asta la tadre, i me vo ir agora mesmo i si eya me demanda eksplikasyones por kualo vine presto a kaza, le vo dezir ke me eskarinyi i vine en kaza por yevarmela a pasear. Bravo, Maurice! Buena te la pensates, esto endo[71] en vista."

I sin dešar a Maurice pronunsyar ninguna otra palavra, el puso su chapeo en la kavesa i se fue a kaza.

Kapitulo 5

Madame Žulyet ya era sigura de loke aviya pensado ma eya keriya mas muncho asigurarse si loke aviya pensado era verdad. Eya se pensava ke manera azer para goler[72] la boka de su marido kuando subito la puerta de su kamareta se avryo i Armand entro en sonryendo.

"Me estas metyendo en kuydado! Esklamo Žulyet, a estas oras ke buškas en kaza?"

"Te olvidates, mi kerida, ke estamos en la luna de myel? Me eskarinyi i vine por verte."

"Kaliya ke vinyeras una ora mas presto, ivas a ver aki una buena pandomima."

"Ke uvo? Algun fuego uvo adentro de kaza?"

"Fuego no uvo, ma uno vino aki para amatar su flamasyon."

"Amatar su flamasyon? Algun ombre vino aki?"

"Ğustamente, uno de tus sinseros amigos, ke lo tyenes komo un ermano."

"Ken es este?"

"Tu amigo Maurice."

"Ke echo tyene Maurice aki entre el diya?"

"Yo puedo saverlo? El vino a vižitar i yo lo resivi komo de uso, ma el miseravle, apenas se asento, me deklaro el amor, me dišo ke se esta muryendo por mi, i munchas otras palavras ke yo kede enkantada[73] al sentirlas."

"Tu ke le dišites?"

"Lo mande kon palos del dyavlo."

Armand aziya semežansa de meterse a pensar i Žulyet kontinuava:

"Esto es ke veas loke son los amigos, akeos amigos ke tu tyenes por muy sinseros. Ma la kulpa no esta en eyos, esta en ti."

"En mi? Ke kulpo yo?"

"Siguro, tu dizes a todos tus amigos ke te selas de tu mužer, i un marido ke sela a su mužer, al kavo la aze

135

enfastyar[74] porke lo enganye, es ğustamente la primera arma ke el se atrevyo a ronğarme. Apenas entro, el empeso en estos terminos:"

'Vos tomo en grande pyedad, Madame Žulyet, vos [sos] una mužer tan linda, tan ermoza, tan grasyoza, tener un marido seloso, esto es mui desagradavle. Dinyad akordar vuestra amistad a mi i vivireš bastante kontente.'

I en dizyendo ansi el me mostro la vida dulse ke va bivir kon el i la vida desastroza ke so aparežada[75] a bivir kon un marido selozo."

"I tu, ke le dišites?"

"Ke le va dezir? Le diše ke no supo batalyar la puerta ğusta i ke deviya ir a otro lugar. Ainda tengo 15 diyas de kazada, si yo tendre 15 anyos i mesmo 150 anyos, nunka buškariya azer traisyon a mi marido."

Armand empeso a reirse, i Žulyet, keryendo empesar a entrar al kamino ke eya keriya konoser, se le aserko del marido, lo tomo a fišugar[76] i apanyandolo en sus brasos le dize:

"Dime Armand, te vo demandar una koza, me vas a dezir?"

"Byen siguro."

"Ma si una koza de no dezir."[77]

"Entre un marido i una mužer kerensyozos no deve aver ningun sekreto, yo lo se. Deves saverlo tu, i loke tu saves devo saverlo yo, si tu amistad es sinsera sigun la miya."

"La verdad ke te diga, te sospechi! La forma ke Maurice estava avlando i ke las miradas de pyedad ke me estava ronğando, kon sus sonrizas burleskas, me izo sospechar ke era metido de tu parte para provarme."

"Por esto es loke no kižites atorgar?"

"Esta palavra tomala atras, Armand! Tu dišites ke me amas, i una ves ke me amas deves dezirme si loke pensi es verdad. Te lo digo i te lo dire syempre. No solo kon Maurice, ma kon vente otros komo Maurice me puedes provar. Nunka buškare a azer traisyon a mi marido."

"Mira Žulyet, Maurice no es metido miyo, otro ke el miseravle kižo buškar a echarte en la red kontemplando tu ermozura. I para asigurarte de loke te digo, te azi remarkar ke ainda no tengo sospecho de tu onestidad, nuestro amor es freska[78], y si mesmo seriya un marido el mas negro ainda es presto para azerme traisyon. Portanto, ya te lo diše, una ves, te lo dire i sigunda[79], las mužeres no soš negras ma soš mui pyadozas, ay entre nosotros ombres gwerkos ke saven rovar el korason kon sus falsas prometas i sus falsas ǧuras[80]. I la mas rezistyente mužer, el korason se le avlanda."

"Esto todo a ti te lo dišeron, i es tu ke lo entendites?"

"La praktika dela vida me lo izo entender."

"Falsa idea! Todas las mužeres no son unas, komo no lo son tambyen todos los ombres.Te lo digo i te lo dire. Yo so onesta i te rogo de no selarme, porke es el selo ke aze ovligar ala mužer a koromperse."

"I tu, en esto estas yerada."

"No Sinyor, yo tengo razon. Enfin, seremos la kuestyon! Agora ke ya vinites la manyana, keres komer meso ǧorno[81] en kaza?"

"Ǧustamente, es por esto ke vine."

"Vaya!" esklamo la mužer en sonryendo, i yamando ala mosa, le ordeno de aparežar el pranso.

Kapitulo 7 (*Sic*, Debería ser 6)

Un ombre puede fyar al otro todo loke kere, oro, plata, ǧoliya[82], kazas etc, ma kuando se trata de azerlo beke[83] de una mužer e inspektor de su komporto, kada ombre deve pensar antes de azerlo, i saver byen eskožer la persona para esta misyon. Esto mo lo embezamos[84] ǧustamente de esta istorya, sigun nuestros lektores ya lo van a ver.

Kuando Maurice salyo dela kaza de Žulyet dela misyon ke Armand le aviya enkargado, el no saliya sigun aviya entrado. El teniya una koza demaziya! Esta koza era el amor ke el resentiya por Žulyet. Munchas vezes el aviya entrado i salido ala kaza de Armand, i su mužer le paresiya una simple dama. Ma esta ves topando frente kon frente kon Žulyeta, konversando mas demazisa[85] sovre echos mas importantes, Maurice topava en Žulyeta una linda mužer ke le kavakava[86] el korason, el aviya ido por tomarla, ma su korason le deziya de tomarla i una bos saliya de su korason ke le desiya:

"Esta es la mužer ke tu keres! Esta es la mužer ke tu tyenes menester."

Es por esto ke el esperava kon dispasensia el retorno de Armand a su buro.

"Si la mužer guadra el sekreto de mi de

Entrega 3

klarasyon[87] de amor, esto prova ke eya ya kere i ke komo todas las mužeres, devi un poko insistir. Ma si eya deskuvre a su marido todo lo ke yo le avli, alora sera muy difisil para reušir. En todo kavzo, yo devo a todo presyo alcansarla. Eya inflamo mi korason y me esto muryendo por eya. Deša veremos! Ke venga Armand, es de su repuesta ke yo devo desidarme[88] ke es lo ke devo yo azer."

I nuestro žoven Maurice, kemado de amor por Žulyeta, empeso a esperar kon dispasensya el aribo de Armand.

Ma este ultimo, sigun ya lo vimos, se aviya kedado a komer en kaza, i myentras dos oras y medya nuestro žoven Maurice esperava kon dispasensia sin komer del todo, enchendo i vasyando syempre sigaro ensima de sigaro.

Ğusto tres oras se pasavan kuando subito la puerta se avriya i Armand entrava en sonryendo.

"Ke ḥaber? Salyo loke diše yo?"

"Ğustamente, despues ke eya me konto todo lo ke tu dišites, eya entendyo tambyen ke sos metido de mi i ke fuites por p[r]ovarla."

"I tu, lo atorgates?"

"Del todo, yo me ize enteramente del ke no tengo avizo, i fui hasta yamarte kobardo delantre mi mužer."

"Izites muy bueno, porke si tu le atorgavas, yo no iva tener mas koraže de ir por tu kaza."

"Esto ya paso, agora kualo vamos azer?"

"Kualo keres azer?"

"Provar a mi mužer, a todo presyo yo devo saver si es onesta."

Maurice se metyo a pensar i pokos sigundos despues el respondyo:

"Agora ke tu mužer ya supo ke yo no fui de tu parte por provarla, keres ke vaya otra ves a kontinuar mi amor?"

"Tu resiviras la mesma repuesta de la primera vižita."

"Ya es verdad, ma tu no saves la vida delas mužeres. La mas ližera mužer nunka atorgariya a todo loke le demandas. Es a misura e ir avlando, de ir arogando, ke se pervyene[89] a apanyar el korason de una mužer."

"Krees ke tyenes razon en loke estas avlando?"

"Siguro."

"Ma yo kreiya ke mandar a otro seriya mižor."

"Del todo, porke si el sigundo no reušo, vas a mandar a un tresero, si el tresero no reušo, vas a mandar un kuatrino y un diya te va kombinar un amigo un poko mas boš bogas[90], i le va deskuvrir a tu mužer loke tu estas azyendo. Ma kuando es uno solo ke va munchas vezes, en kada ves ke va, se avre un poko mas, i ansi tyene

139

esperansa de konoser el korason de eya."

"Tyenes razon, esto de akordo en este razonamyento, entra i sale komo keres a mi kaza, basta ke me sepas provarme si mi mužer es onesta, o no."

Kapitulo 8

Ya puedeš kreer la alegriya de Maurice en tomando lisensya de Armand de ir vižitar kada diya a Žulyeta.

"Entrando y saliyendo ala kaza de Žulyeta yo esto siguro de reušir! Es verdad ke en los primeros momentos, una mužer no atorga tan presto ma a mizura de ir marteandola[91], esto siguro de reušir."

El se espartyo de Armand prometyendole de ir al otro diya a vižitar a su mužer i se fue ala kaye komo un loko por pensar ke plano tomar a reušir en este echo.

Despues de pasar por su memorya munchos prožetos y planos, el se akodro de su amigo Rišard.

"Este amigo puedriya serme de grande utilita[92], deziya el. "Este bravo Rišard save trokar dyez amores en dyez puntos. Yo ire onde el i tomare unas kuantas lisyones esta manyana."

La desizyon tomada, Maurice iva derechamente onde Rišard por komunikarle loke konosemos.

El žoven Rišard era el ižo de un riko bankyero ke saviya komerse las paras[93] sin espanto de escaparsen[94] porke su padre, despues ke era bien riko, lavorava cada dya i toda la ganansya pasava a kuento de su ižo regalado, ke veniya solo dos o tres oras al diya a la banka.

El diya ke Maurice se aviya desidado a ir a vižitar a Rišard, este ultimo era muy pensativle. El se pensava ke ya se aviya enfastyado[95] de todos los visyos, ke las aktrises le veniyan a kostar munchas sumas, i ke ala fin del kuento estas aktrises no eran a el solo ke konosiyan. El se desidava a kazarse, ma no kon una mužer ležitima, porke estava siguro ke de esta mužer tambyen se iva esfastyar. El keriya desidarse a tomar una metres[96] ke konoseriya solo a el.

El pensava a esto, kuando vido aserkarse de el a su amigo Maurice en saludando:

"Bon ǧorno, Rišard."

"Bon ğorno, Maurice."

"Vine rogarte un plazir, o por mižor dezir, un konsežo."

"De kualo se trata? Kuestyon de mužer?"

"Ğustamente."

"Avla, veremos, i tu sufres de la mesma ḥazinura[97] miya."

"Kon una chika diferensya. Tu estas p[r]opuendyendo[98] alkansar ala ke keres, ma yo no."

"Kon la moneda todo se alkansa."

"Todo no, mi kerido, ğustamente yo dariya todo mi kapital por alkansar a esta mužer ke yo amo."

"Eya es ermoza?"

"Mui ermoza! Ma... mui onesta, mui fidela a su marido."

"Ke es loke keres tu ke te konseže yo?"

"Kualo azer por pueder alkansarla."

"Pedirla cada diya, dezirle ke te estas muryendo por eya, rogarle, suplikarle, finke se le ablanda el korason y te atorga. Me puedes dezir ken es esta mužer?"

"La mužer de Armando el nuestro."

"Ay! Ke kazo antes 15 dyas?"

"Ğustamente."

"Es una ermoza mužer! Tyenes razon. Esto ke te diše deves azer."

"Ma no saves loke ay enmedyo."

"Ke koza?"

En kortas palavras, Maurice konto a Rišard loke nuestros lektores ya konosen i el rifuzo kategoriko de Žulyet.

Esta deklarasyon metiya en penseryo a Rišard ke se deziya entre si.

"Na[99] un buen remedyo ala ke yo esto buškando. Yo konosko mi kapasidad i esto siguro de reušir."

Levantando la kaveza, el diše a Maurice:

"Keres prezentarme tu a esta dama?"

"Para kualo?"

"Por embezarte[100] ke formas se enganya una mužer."

"I si me la tomates de la mano?"

"Esto no te ago, ma puede ser ke te demando parte de

142

la ganansya."

"Dešame provar una o dos vezes otras, y despues, si no reusko[101], ya demando tu konkorso."

"¡Sea!"

Maurice saluda su amigo, sale ala kaye, i se va derechamente onde perdyo la alguža[102].

Arivando serka la puerta de kaza, el se detyene en dizyendo:

"Uy! No va ir una sigunda ves. Lo va dešar para manyana."

Akea noche el la pasa aki i alya espera[103] kon dispasensya el aribo del diya. Y kuando ya aze kuento ke Armand ya saldriya de kaza, el se va a vižitar a Madame Žulyet. Esta ultima lo resive kon un tono mas seryoso de syempre, i l [e] mostra lugar para asentar.

Maurice se asenta en tomando la palavra.

"Eskuzad me[104], Madame, del deranžo ke vos esto kavzando, mi difunto padre me deziya ke el tyempo es la mas grande melizina de todas las yagas. Kon el tyempo todo se alkansa. En estas 24 oras ke pasaron no pensaryaš un poko por este esklavo parado delantre de vos i ke se esta muryendo por alkansarvos?"

"No pensi nunka a vos, para ke me vinyeras al tino."

"Portanto, Madame, deves tener un poko pyedad por mi; va salir loko por vos, i un rifuzo de vuestra parte meteriya mi vida en perikolo."

Žulyet sonreiya kon burla en respondyendo:

"Esta arma no fyere[105] mi korason porke yo la konosko de munchos ombres. No, Sinyor Maurice, ni munchos otros komo Sinyor Maurice no pueden gastar mi onor.Es por esto ustamente ke vos vo rogar un plazir ke me agas."

"Ordenad, Madame, vuestro esklavo esta dispuesto a todos vuestros[106] ordenes."

"No tengo ningun orden a darvos, loke tengo de dezirvos es ke, si vas a venir a mi kaza, deves venir onestamente komo veniyas antes. Ma si tenes idea, en kada ves ke vas a venir, de buškar a gastar el onor de mi marido y el miyo, me azes plazir si no venes mas."

"Me estas ronğando de vuestra kaza? Madame![107]"

"Yo no vos esto ronğando, ma vos keres ke vos ronğen. Ya vos diše ke no ay ningun provecho en mi, yo so una mužer kazada, vivyendo una vida kerensyosa kon mi marido, i nunka meti en tino a vender el onor. Es a vos de eskožer el kamino."

"Ma, Madame Žulyet, no me estas kreendo. Vos amo! Vos adoro! Dinyad tener un poko de pyedad por mi."

"Antes ke tenga por vos, kale ke tenga por mi."

"Alora? Yo devo esperar ainda."

"Esperar i dezesperar mesmo[108]."

"Ma Madame, vos estas vengando de mi!"

"Kitaldo[109] del tino, Sinyor Maurice. En mi no tenes ningun provecho. Batalyad otra puerta."

I Žulyeta se levantava i sin saludar a Maurice se retirava.

144

Kapitulo 9

Dešaremos por el momento a Maurice penar en baldes i vayamos a ver al žoven Rišard loke el va azer despues de la konversasyon ke el tuvo kon Maurice.

Ya dešimos ke el visyo de korer detras de mužeres lo aviya enfastyado i ke el dezeava atarse kon una sola mužer por syempre.

La deklarasyon de Maurice le aziya akodrar la ermozura de la mužer de Armand ke el aviya visto una sola ves i ke aviya kontemplado su ermozura sin pueder nada azer, en pensando ke se tratava de la mužer de un amigo. Ma kuando Maurice vino a avlarle el se olvido de este dever i empeso a pensar en loke el keriya alkansar.

Un momento, el keriya azerle una karta en inchendola de akeos byervos ke azen menear los pelos dela karne. Ma byen presto, el troko de idea i se desidyo de ir azer una vižita a esta dama ke la konosiya solo de una ves ke la aviya visto el diya de su boda.

El se desida en vista i akea mesma tadre, antes ke Maurice fuera, el kor[yo] ala kaza de Armand.

La mosa le avre la puerta, el prezenta su karta de vižita i sinko puntos despues, Rišard ya era enel salon de resepsyon de Madame Žulyet. Esta ultima le aziya un resibo muy galante i lo aziya asentar en un riko fotolyo[110].

"Eskuzadme, Madame, del deranžo ke vos vo kavzar," deziya Rišard, "no tengo la konosensya kon vos ke solo el diya dela boda, ma tengo un echo a skomunikarvos[111] ke me ovliga a venir vižitarvos."

"De kualo se trata, Sr.?"

"Vine dezirvos ke un mansevo de 28 anyos esta en perikolo de morir, i ke es solo vos ke tenes la melezina."

"Ariyas bueno si vos eksplikavas un poko mas klaro, no esto entendyendo."

"Ma! Madame! Kon ke koraže avlarvos, vos ǧuro ke no se! Del primer momento ke vos enkontre, el diya de

145

vuestro kazamyento, mi korason se ḥarvo por vos, yo no se loke es ni komer, ni dormir. Myentras 15 diyas, yo tuve pasensya por no azer traisyon a un amigo miyo komo Armand. Ma oy, la pasensya desbordo, i vine echarme a vuestros pyes a ke tengas pyedad por mi. Mi vida esta en perikolo, y un rifuso de vuestra parte seriya kondanarme al desespero i al suisidyo."

I Rišard izo semežansa de kerer yorar.

Žulyet mirava kon atansyon al nuevo venido, i deziya entre si:

"Na otro un gwerko ke vino a marearme!"

Enderechandose en su lugar, eya empeso a sonreir kon burla, y respondyo:

"Komo el mundo troko, todos los amigos devinyeron[112] falsos. Vos disites endagora ke mi marido es vuestro amigo, i kon ke koraže vos atreveš a arevatar el onor de uno ke dizes [s]er vuestro amigo."

"Tenes razon, Madame, es un krimen ke esto azyendo, mas kualo ke aga? Mi korason se ḥarvo de vos, yo buski munchas vezes a olvidarme, no pude. Es el desespero ke me ovligo a venir batalyar la puerta de vuestro korason pyadozo."

"Batalyates una puerta muy yerrada! Mi korason despues ke no es blando, es mui duro. Yo teniya menester un cliyente para vender mi korason, ya lo topi, ya lo vendi i oy, afuera de mi marido, ninguno otro puede apatronarse de el."

"I kereš por vuestro kavzo ke un mansevo se muera?"

"Ninguno se muere por una mužer, basta ke tenga meolyo. Si es loko, no se."

"Ma Madame, vos olvidates ke el amor tyene una fuerte lansa para kondenarlo a morir."

"Es para akeos ke se keren servir de la lansa. Ma akeos ke saven byen ǧuzgar las kozas, pueden mui byen entender ke en un echo ke no ay provecho, no deven tener esperansa."

"Vos ǧuro, Madame, ke yo no kreiya ke no aviyas a tener un poko de pyedad."

"Pyedad tengo yo por los proves i por los ḥazinos[113]...
ma... por akeos ke keren manchar mi onor devo tener
pyedad emprimero de mi, despues de otro."

"Ma, Madame, kreedme, vos rogo, esto kondenado."

"Poko me importa! Si sos loko andadvos al espital[114].
Puede ser vos ḥarvariyas de mi, i,

Entrega 4

por kalmar vuestro amor, buškates a deklararlo. Izites
muy bueno, puede ser tendriyas algun provecho, pero una
ves ke viteš ke no ay provecho, deveš trokar de idea."

"Ma, Madame, no lo esto puedyendo."

"Lo puedeš muy byen, Sinyor Rišard, vos venites aki a
kavsa ke vos estaš muryendo por mi, i no vos keres morir.
I ahora dezid ke una ves ke no ay provecho, i no me kero
morir, no devo morirme, i ansi no vos mueriras! Me
parese ke no so yo la unika mužer en el mundo, ay munchas otras mižor de mi, deklarad el amor kon una de eyas
i vereš ke apunto la amistad ke tenes por mi la tendres
por eya."

Rišard no se dešava konvenser a esta repuesta, i keriya
mas kontinuar a avlar, ma Žulyeta no le dešava el tyempo
en kontinuando.

"No vos kanseš en baldes, Sinyor Rišard. Es verdad ke
puede ser ke antes de kazar, yo tuve algunas aventuras
ma agora mi korason ya se vendyo a uno i no puede
merkarlo otro. Kon esto, vo[s] lo repito. Puedeš venir aki
a vižitar en kualidad de amigo, ma nunka kon mal pen-
samyento porke no teneš provecho."

"Por oy, yo no vos rongo de kaza, ma si una otra ves en
vinyendo, me avlas de nuevo de vuestro amor, vos digo de
agora ke vos mostrare la puerta."

A esta repuesta, Rišard no topava mas kualo dezir i el
se levantava por saludar.

Keryendo espandir la mano, Žulyeta le dize:

"No ay menester, Sinyor Rišard, esto ke se toma una

salata para avrir la gana es kuando ya esta la komida detras. Una ves ke de mi no teneš ningun provecho, el tokar la mano vos ara mas danyo ke provecho.

I el povre Rišard se retira, triste i abatido, no avyendo reušido por la primera ves, a enganyar una mužer.

Kedando sola, Žulyeta se empesa a reir komo una kriatura en esklamando:

"Kuryoso mundo, kuando era muchacha, i ke estava dezeando kazarme, ninguno me se aserkava por deklararme el amor. Agora ke ya kazi, todos keren korer detras de mi. Ma es en baldes. No tyenen provecho. El dever de una mužer kazada es de ser onesta. Kavzo kontraryo, las kriaturas ke nasen salen korompidas[115]. I despues, una amistad de marido i mužer kuando no ay amar[116] a otro. Kuando uvo amar[117] a un sigundo, guay ke le vino, el tresero i el kuarto ya estan despues, i si no vyenen es la mužer ke los buska."

"No! No!... No devo vender mi korason a ninguno. Yo devo bivir onesta i morir onesta!"

Kapitulo 10

Kuando Rišard saliya dela kaza de Žulyeta, el no saviya kualo azer. Kuando el aviya ido ayi el aviya ido simplemente por echar ala pesca una mužer. Ma apenas el se topava enfrente de Žulyeta, empesava a konversar, la dulse konversasyon le aziya kemar su korason i en kada ves ke la mužer de Armand refusava a su dezeo, su korason se le inflamava, i kuando el saliya de ayi, el era el amorozo syego de la linda Žulyeta.

Auntando a esto el kaprisyo del rifuso, el keriya a todo presyo alkansarla, al riziko[118] de azer gastos lokos, ma komo puedriya el parvenir una ves ke Žulyeta le deziya ke no puediya vender su korason a otro?

El kaminava komo un loko por la kaye, abokado e pensativle, sin azer del todo atansyon a akeos ke lo saludavan. Kaminava los ožos enbažo, el se harvo subito kon un ombre en el braso i el levanto la kavesa por demandar pardon.

"Este karar[119] de okupado estas, Rišard?" le demando Žakomo, un amigo de Rišard ke era akel ke le aviya harvado el braso.

"Ah! Amigo, no me demandes. Tengo en la kavesa un penseryo tan fuerte ke no me esto puedyendo debrolyar[120]."

"De kualo se trata?"

"Ah! Žakomo! No konoses byen mi vida, i la manera ke yo la giyo[121]. Aze serka dies anyos ke yo me engrandesko en visyos, i nunka tengo atado amor a una ninya. Malorozamente[122], en estos dyas me apanyi kon una mužer, i me esto muryendo por eya.

"Morido si kere [s]?[123] Tu tyenes una buena posisyon i la puedes muy byen tomarla por mužer."

"Malorozamente, no, eya es kazada!"

"Kazada!"

"Si, kon un amigo miyo."

"Alora, komo te atreves a amarla?"

"Komo me atrevo?... No saves komo en el amor no ay limito? Yo la vide, me plazyo, la ami."

"I ya le deklarates el amor?"

"Ǧustamente."

"Esto si kere un koraže partikolar."

"El amor trae todo. Del primer momento ke ḥarvi de eya, me desidi a azer todos los sakrifisyos, i yo me fui onde eya kon intensyon de prometerle moneda porke me kontentara. Ma eya no aksepto. Antes de konoser el eskopo de mi vižita, eya me izo un kalurozo resivo, loke me izo enkoražar a empesar a avlar. Ma apena empesi en la konversasyon, eya tambyen troko de tono, me izo seryosa, i vyendo ke yo kontinuava en mis avlas, eya me mostro la puerta."

"Primera ves ke le avlates fue?"

"Ǧustamente."

"Ainda tyenes esperansa. Las mužeres, partikolarmente las kazadas, kon primera i kon sigunda ves, eyas no akseptan un amor, es menester de korer detras de eyas, empesar kon merkarle regalos, i a misura de ir frekuentando, deklararle el amor kon pasensya i no de un golpe."

"Ya es verdad, ma agora ke ya lo ize, es un echo ke no se vyene reparar."

"En todo kavzo, merka un kolye[124] de perla[125] i yevaselo manyana, yo tengo grande esperansa ke el kolye va azer grande koza."

"Tyenes razon de avlar ansi[126]. Tu no vites el refuso kategoriko ke eya me izo."

"Esto es nada. Kuanto mas dura es al prinsipyo, mas blanda se aze despues. Aze loke te diše i vas a ver."

"Vo provar loke me estas dizyendo ma no kreo ke va pueder reušir."

"Si tu no reušes, es ke yo no se nada en el mundo."

Los dos amigos se desparten[127], i Rišard se va derechamente onde un bižutyero[128] ke el konosiya, i le dize de darle un kolye de perla.

El ǧolyero le mostra munchos kampyones[129], i a la fin el amorozo žoven eskože uno, i lo merka moayar[130] en dando el importe i dizyendole:

"Si a mi mužer le agrado, lo va detener. El montante ya te pagi. Si no le plazyo, te lo vo a traer, i me vas a dar el montante atras."

El akordo es echo, i Rišard toma el kolye i se va a su kaza por lyevarselo el otro diya.

Kapitulo 11

Dešaremos a Rišard por el momento kon su kolye, azerse munchas ilusyones, i retornemos a la kaza de Žulyeta, por ver ayi tambyen kualo es loke se va pasar.

Nuestros lektores se akodraran por siguro loke Žulyeta aviya indivinado kuando Maurice aviya venido a deklararle el amor; la manera de ke eya aviya golido[131] la boka de su marido.

Kuando Rišard vino i se fue, apunto eya empeso de nuevo a sospechar i kreer ke era el marido ke lo aviya mandado por provarla por sigunda ves. Eya se empesa a meter en kolora[132] i a eskrožir dyentes, i a la noche, kuando el desdichado del marido vyene, eya empesa a gritarlo[133] i a dezirle:

"Oyates Armand, si no tyenes confiansa en mi, no me tengas por mužer. Yo no puedo mas sufrir tus provas. Ya te diše munchas veses ke yo so onesta, ke ningun ombre me puede enganyar i ke nunka buškare a gastar el onor de mi marido. Ke dezmodramyento es este, de ir mandando ğente para ke me proven!"

"Ken mando ğente?" Esklamo Armand ke en verdad no teniya avizo de nada.

"Ken va mandar? Tu! Ayer fue a Maurice; oy fue a Rišard. Manyana veremos ke sampavlo[134] va ser."

"Rišard? Kual Rišard?"

"Tu amigo, el ižo del avocato."

"El ruvyo?"

"Ğustamente."

"Te ğuro, Žulye[t], ke no tengo avizo. Si keres ke te avle lo ğusto, ayer a Maurice es yo ke lo mandi, ma a Rišard, no tengo del todo avizo."

"I komo vyene el aki? Komo puede el enkoražarse a venir aki y deklararme el amor, sin konoserme de mui serka?"

"Žulyet, te ğuro en mi onor ke no tengo avizo. Kuando

152

vino el?"

"Oy mesmo."

"I ke te dišo?"

"Ke me va dezir? El diskurso ke azes[135] todos los ombres enfrente las mužeres. Te amo, te adoro, me esto muryendo por ti, y munchos otros byervos peludos y pepitudos[136], nasidos para enganyar alas mužeres."

"I tu ke le dišites?"

"Ke le va[137] dezir? Le diše ke venga amanyana."

"Kualo? Ke koza? Lo invitates para amanyana?"

"Loko! Es posivle? I si lo inviti, te va[138] dezir ke lo inviti? Yo lo ronǧi kon palos del diavlo i le diše ke no se atreva mas a pizar mi kaza."

"Muy bueno izites, bravo! Me esto konvensyendo ke sos una mužer onesta!"

Armand deziya esto kon un tono mui afavle, ma en su korason un otro penseryo le pasava por su memorya, i el kontinuava a avlar en estos terminos.

"Kerida Žulyet, no alargaremos la konversasyon. Yo no te provi, ni tengo mas menester de provarte. Ya entendi ke sos una mužer onesta. Solamente, te dire ke loke vine temprano es simplemente por dezirte ke tengo menester de irme esta tadre a un randevu[139] por un echo importante."

"Ke echo importante es? Topar otro amigo para mandarlo ke me prove?"

"No, mi kerida, es de un echo ke creo ay de ganar muncha moneda."

"Una ves ke es ansi, vate, ma no tadres."

Kon grande dispasensya Armand resiviya esta repuesta de su mužer i, en vista, el se ronǧava ala kaye en dizyendo entre si:

"Na otra una okasyon ke me se prezenta i ke no devo dešarla. Rišard deklaro el amor a mi mužer. El es un ombre kapache i yo devo enkargarlo a ke kontinue este amor i ke prove a mi mužer."

El empesa a apresurar sus pasos i dyes puntos despues el ya era en el otel onde Rišard dormiya cada noche.

"Senyor Rišard es prezente?" demanda el al portalero."

"Si Sinyor, ğustamente agora vyene de[140] venir."

"Vos rogo dezirme el no. dela kamara."

"No. 14."

Armand suve en koryendo la eskalera i ḥarva ala puerta del no. 14.

Un grito responde: "Entrad".

I Armand avre la puerta i entra adyentro.

Rišard es asentado ensima de una kanape[141] egzaminando el kolye.

"Bon suar[142], Rišard! esklama Armand en entrando."

La kolor de kara de Rišard se aze en munchas kolores, kuando ve venir al marido de Žulyeta. Para kualo veniya el?... Su mužer le tendriya avlado alguna koza?

Sin del todo azer ver su intensyon, Rišard lo resive kon muncha korteziya en espandyendole la mano.

"Sea byen venido, Armand. Komo fue ke venites a verme? Del diya ke kazates te olvidates enteramente de los amigos."

"Yo me olvidi delos amigos, ma tu tambyen te olvidates ke esto en la luna de myel. Un rezen kazado pensa syempre a su mužer en los primeros meses."

"Sea. No tengo sido kazado por konoser la valor. En todo kavzo, tu vižita me aze meter en grande penseryo. Kualo te pušo a venir aki a vižitarme en una tadrada dela luna de myel?"

"Ya se ke te aviya a maravear, ma vine a rogarte un plazir."

"Un plazir? De mi? Tu sos mas riko de mi i mas potente de mi. Ke plazir te puedo yo azerte a ti?"

"Un plazir muy grande."

"Algun emprestito?"

"No, grasyas al Dyo, ya tengo moneda muncha."

"I kualo, alora?"

"Syente[143], Rišard, mi mužer me konto ke tu estuvites oy demanyana en mi kaza, i ke le deklarates el amor."

En esta pregunta Rišard empesava a temblar en dešando kontinuar al marido de Žulyeta.

154

"No tembles i no te espantes, todos fuimos mansevos i todos konosimos la valor del amor. Puede ser la vites en algun balo, te plazyo, la amates. Solamente kero ke me digas la verdad. Ke te respondyo eya?"

"Ke me va responder? Repuesta negativa i akompanyada de ronğamyento de kaza."

"Ya me estas respondyendo ğusto?"

"Te ğuro. Pura verdad."

"Una ves ke es ansi, el plazir ke te vo rogar es akel de kontinuar en tu echo, a kondisyon de no azerme traisyon."

"Kualo? Ke koza?"

"Loke sentites. Kero ke kontinues a deklarar el amor kon mi mužer por ver si te va atorgar."

"Para kualo es esto?"

"Yo kero provarla!"

"Bovo! Mužer se prova? Nunka! Una ves ke ya estas mirando ke ya es onesta, dešala ala natura. Para kualo punğarla[144] i azerla entrompeser?"

"Para saver si es onesta."

"Es una lokura loke estas azyendo. Kale ke sea ke no le tyenes amistad a tu mužer."

"La amo mucho."

"Una ves ke la amas, kale ke tengas konfiansa."

Entrega 5

Es ğustamente la kontra, porke la amo muncho es ke me esto selando."

"Idea vana! No se ğoga kon una mužer."

"Algun danyo tyenes tu? Yo kero ke la proves, tanto mas ke eya ya era sospechando ke es yo ke te enkargi por provarla."

"Estas buškando un kamino para bivir dezrepozado. Veḥamente[145] dezirte, es porke me ḥarvi mui muncho de tu mužer, ke yo tuve el koraže de ir a tu kaza i de deklararme. Su repuesta negativa me aziya pedrer toda

155

esperansa, i esto mesmo desidado a no mas batalyar la puerta de tu kaza, por no azer la asnidad esta el kavo[146]. Ma... una ves ke tu keres, por plazirte, kontinuare. Ma estate siguro ke tu mužer no va akseptar a mi oferta, esto es visto i revisto, i yo lo remarki desde ayer."

"Yo tambyen ya se esto, ma kero asigurarme mas muncho."

"Alora, yo ire otra ves manyana, i de loke vo azer te vo yevar avizo."

"Me lo prometes?"

"Te lo prometo, kerido Armand."

"Alora, yo me vo."

I, levantandose, Armand saludava a Rišard i se retirava.

Kapitulo 12

Ya puedeš kreer la alegriya de Rišard en sintyendo la konversasyon de Armand por irse la sigunda ves para ver a Žulyeta. El se estava muncho pensando komo iva ir a verla, por no ser ke su marido se topara en kaza, i ke Žulyeta le deskuvryera a su marido la sigunda venida, ma esta deklarasyon de Armand le aziya dar grande koraže por ir a verla, sigunda ves... auntando a esto el empleo del kolye. Esto le dava esperansa de pueder reušir.

Kon grande dispasensya, el espera la noche entera, i kuando ve venir la manyana, se arapa[147] i se peyna, i kore ande Žulyeta a las oras 11.

La ermoza Žulyeta ya se aviya olvidado de todo loke le aviya pasado el diya de antes. Es verdad ke la tadre, eya se aviya peleado kon su marido porke aviya kreido ke era un otro amigo ke le aviya mandado para provarla, ma kuando despues en la noche, el marido veniya i se razonava, Armand le dava a entender komo no aviya nada, i ansi, eya se reposava i olvidava enteramente toda la konversasyon de Rišard.

Su enkanto fue byen grande en vyendolo venir el sigundo dya. Eya lo resivyo un poko mas yelada[148] i nuestro žoven Rišard, sin del todo deskoražarse, se inklinava delantre de eya en disyendole:

"Madame, vos rogo de eskužarme del deranžo ke vos kavza mi vižita ayer. Pasando por el bazar de los ǧolyeros vide un kolye de perla, me plazyo bastante i lo merki a vuestra intensyon, Madame."

"Pena en baldes, Sinyor Rišard, un kolye de perla no puede arevatar mi onor. Yo vos rogo de no embabokarvos[149] en kozas ke no se pueden realizar. La repuesta ke yo vos di ayer es la mesma repuesta de oy. Por la ultima ves vos digo, no puedo vender el korason a ninguno. El apartyene solo a mi marido, i vos rogo de no mas venir por aki, porke sin tener vos ningun provecho, me kavzariyaš muncho danyo. Mi marido es muy selozo, i si el azardo trušo a ke el venga, en loke vos estaš aki, yo sere pedrida."

"Si vuestro marido vos deša, yo vos tomo."

"Munchas grasyas, Sinyor, ma para azer este transferto, es el desonor ke ǧugara en medyo. Mi difunto padre me dešo komo toda erensya, onor de familya, i este onor no devo nunka gastarlo."

"No se kualo respondervos, Madame, a este grande kaprisyo vuestro. Yo se ke las mužeres son mui piadozas[150], i kuando se trata de no dešar morir a un mansevo ke se esta muryendo por eya."

"Ǧustamente en esto teneš yerro, akeas mužeres ke tyenen pyedad por akel ke se kere morir por eya, es porke tyenen pyedad tambyen en el regalo ke van a tomar de sus amante[151], o ke ya estan auzadas. Buškad una de eyas, i tendra muy presto pyedad de vos."

Rišard no se deskoraža a esta repuesta i el respondiya kon muncho koraže:

"No sea, madame, ke vos esta paresyendo ke es vuestro marido ke me embyo a provarvos i es por esto ke no kereš apiadarvos de mi? Vos ǧuro, Madame, ke teneš[152] grande yerro. Yo vos amo de puro korason i teneš grande yerro de todo loke estariyas pensando sovre este sužeto[153]."

"Sinyor Rišard, no vayas dando vueltas para echarme ala red. No teneš del todo provecho de mi. Vos rogo de retirarvos. Por la ultima ves, vos esto rogando kon buenas, ma si insistes ainda, vo ser ovligado[154] de mostrarvos la puerta."

I en dizyendo estas palavras Žulyeta kontinuava:

"I el kolye, daldo a akea ke va kerer kontinuar[155] vuestro dezeo i no a mi."

Rišard se deskoražava enteramente i el se levantava, saludava ala mužer de Armand sin espandirle la mano i se retirava.

Kapitulo 13

Kuando Rišard saliya de la kaza de Žulyet, el era triste i abatido. El aviya amado a Žulyet, i su linda fizyonomiya le aviya kemado el korason. El kaminava komo un entontesido kuando subito, uno lo detyene en dizyendo:

"Ke izites? Reušites?"

Rišard levanta la kaveza i el enkontra a Armand, el marido de Žulyet.

"Deves felisitarte, Armand," esklama Rišard. "Tyenes una mužer onesta."

"De onde lo provates?"

"La mas dura mužer kon un kolye de perla se ablanda. Portanto[156], tu mužer no se kižo ablandar ni kon esto."

"Tu le yevates un kolye de perla?"

"Ğustamente."

"I ke te dišo eya?"

"Me lo ronğo en la kara en dizyendome — 'Si otra ves me avlas de esto, no vos miro en la kara.' —. Tomi a espesiarme mas muncho, eya me ronğo kon palos de diavlo."

"I ke kontas azer agora? No vas a ir mas a mi kaza?"

"Komo ke vaya? Si en esta ves me ronğo kon la boka, ala otra ves me va ronğar kon el palo. Ya saves, Armand, komo yo fui syempre un mansevo ke frekuenti mužeres i ke buški a echarlas ala pesca. Syempre reuši, salvo esta ves. Te asiguro ke deves felisitarte ke tyenes una mužer onesta."

Armand empesava a pensar en la kolye, no keriyendo kreer alo ke Rišard le desiya, i este ultimo kontinuava:

"Vate a kaza, Armand, vate a kaza, i glorifikate ke tyenes una mužer byen onesta!"

Armand se retirava en dešando a Rišard suspirar de remorso[157] y esklamar entre si:

"Yo, Rišard, no pueder parvenir a alkansar a la sola mužer ke yo amo en mi vida?"

I el kontinuava su kamino, syempre abokado[158],

syempre pensativle.

Una bos le izo despertar subito de su embeliko[159] Era Žákomo su amigo ke lo despertava en gritando:

"Ke izites, Rišard? Reušo loke te konseži?"

"Nada, kerido amigo, ni el kolye izo ayre ni mis rogativas ni mis yoros."

"No insistites a rogarle?"

"Mas de loke pensas. Ma eya me mostro la puerta en ordenandome de no ir mas por ayi."

Žakomo kedava enkantado en respondyendo:

"Me puedes prezentarme tu a esta mužer?"

"Komo ke te la prezente una ves ke no me kižo mas resivir en su kaza?"

"Una sola ves si la veo, esto siguro de echarla ala pesca."

Esta repuesta metiya en trovle[160] a Rišard, ke le veniya apunto al tino una idea, i el se apresurava a responder en dizyendole:

"Mira, Žákomo, alado la amistad ke yo tengo por esta mužer, me se rekresyo tambyen la renkor, o por mižor dezir, el kerer tomar vengansa. Yo no te puedo prezentar a esta mužer, ma ya ay un remedyo para ke tu puedes verla, e ir mesmo una o dos vezes a su kaza."

"Ke manera?"

"Te kontare, kuando tu me konsežates ayer de merkar un kolye, yo lo ize en vista i me fui en kaza por egzaminarlo. Ġusto en el momento ke estava kontando las perlas, vide venir subito a mi kamareta al marido de Žulyeta. Ya puedes kreer el espanto ke tuve. Por mui siguro ke el beniya[161] para afearme del komporto ke tuve serka de su mužer, mi enkanto fue byen grande kuando vide ke era ġustamente por una idea kontrarya a loke yo pensi, ke el veniya. El me rogava de kontinuar a ir a su kaza porke el keriya provar la amistad de su mužer. Yo insisti[162] emprimero, i despues aksepti, la misyon. I oy, ġustamente, el va venir a medyo dya a mi kaza por tomar la repuesta i saver ke es loke ize. Si tu vyenes kon mi, yo le dire ke no ize nada, i te presentare a ti komo mas capae de mi. Esto siguro ke Armand va akseptar kon plazir i el propyo te va presentar a su mužer."

"Esta idea es buena. Vamos derechamente a tu kaza i si Armand atorga a ke yo prove la onestidad de su mužer, te va[163] mostrar komo se echa una mužer ala sesta[164] la mas kaprichosa ke fuese."

Los dos amigos se tomavan el braso i se empesavan a ir de parte la kaza de Rišard.

A sus grande enkanto, Armand ya era esperando en la puerta, i su kolor de kara se le demodava en vyendo a Rišard venir kon un otro amigo enǧuntos.

Rišard lo entendiya byen presto esto, ma el no se travava[165] de aserkarse de el i de dezirle:

"Ya me esperava a vuestro enkontro, Sr. Armand. Bon ǧorno, de los sielos parece ke vos keren ayudar sovre el prožeto ke tyenes en tino i ke keres konoser."

Armand se trovlava a loke Rižard le deziya, no keriyendo ke el amigo ke teniya alado supyera de lo ke se tratava, i Rižard kontinuava:

"Antes de todo, kerido, Armand, te prezentare a mi amigo Sr. Žakomo, un žoven muy kapache[166] i ke puede serte de grande utilidad por lo ke keres tu buškar a saver."

Armand se enkantava mas muncho en respondyendo:

"Ya tyene avizo de nuestro echo?"

"Ǧustamente, fui ovligado de dezirselo porke ala verdad ke te diga, yo no fui kapache de reušir."

"No reušites? Ke dize eya?"

"Syempre repuesta negativa, i poko kedo ke eya me iva ronǧar de kaza."

"I kualo puedra azer Sr. Žakomo?"

"Entraremos en kaza, ayi avlamos mas de ancho."

Los tres ombres ke konosemos entravan en kaza. Rišard les dava a kada uno su lugar, i despues de asentarse en el, se aderesava[167] a Armand en dizyendole:

"Mira, Armand, la primera ves ke yo deklari el amor a tu mužer, eya no aksepto del todo i yo me aviya enteramente deskoražado, ke no kontava del todo ir mas por

161

onde eya. El azardo me izo enkontrar a Žakomo, i yo me vide ovligado de deskuvrirle mi amor por Žulyeta. El me konsežo de merkarle un kolye i de ir otra ves. Yo se lo merki, se lo yevi, ma syempre fue la mesma repuesta: refuso kategoriko. Rongar de kaza."

"Ma, komo la primera ves, la sigunda ves yo me deskuvri kon Žakomo, i el me yamo bovo. El me dišo ke si el es prezentado a esta mužer, el save echarla ala peska en el primer enkontro, o lo mas tadre en el sigundo. Apunto ke me dišo esto, yo pensi a ti, no tyenes ke[168] yevarlo una ves ala kaza i prezentarle a tu mužer, el resto sera su echo."

Armand se metyo a pensar en dizyendo entre si.

"Este ombre se tyene de muy kapache i esta siguro de enganyar a mi mužer. Es verdad ke mi mužer rongo dos amores, ma si se apanyo alkavo, eya es de kuero y gweso i se puede muy byen enganyar."

El pasava este penseryo munchas vezes por su memorya, ma... la ambisyon de konoser la onestidad de su mužer, no le dešavan[169] repozado, i el se desirava[170] a provar una otra ves. El levanta la kaveza i se aderesa a Žakomo en dizyendole:

"Vos kreeš kapache de enganyar a una mužer ke se glorifika de ser onesta?"

"Si, Sinyor Armand."

"I kualo kereš ke vos aga para esto?"

"Solo ke me yeves una ves a vuestra kaza a komer i ke me prezentes a vuestra mužer. El resto sera mi echo. Solamente tomad de nota ke mi pago [sera] 5000 frankos[171] para azer esta kapasidad[172]."

"500 frankos? Ke vas a vender para ganar esta suma?"

"Kapachidad, Sr. Armand."

"I si no izites nada?"

"No me vas a dar nada."

"Un poko de reduksyon, si vos plaze. 5000 frankos es muy karo."

"Yo vos ago mižor.Mostradme una ves a vuestra mužer, i despues vos metes en trato. Delos ožos, yo vos se dezir si eya entra en la peska de un ombre o si no entra."

"Esto es mižor. De akordo."

"Byen, agora, ala noche, kuando vas a ir en kaza, vas a dezir a vuestra mužer ke resivites un telegrafo de uno de vuestros amigos de Londra, un amigo muy kerido ke se yama Lord Žorž Frodel. El arivara manyana manyana, i es menester aparežar en kaza un buen pranso porke vo[s] lo vaš a traer a kaza a komer. I manyana, a medyo diya, me yevaš a vuestra kaza. El resto es mi echo."

"I esto estamos de akordo. Yo me vo ir de agora en kaza por informar mi mužer a ke empese de agora los aparežos, i manyana a las oras 11, me esperas aki. Yo vos tomare i vos yevare a mi kaza, desa[173] veremos vuestra kapasidad."

Los dos nuevos amigos se apretavan las manos komo senyal de mostrar ke estan en un komun akordo i se saludavan. Armand se iva enderecho a su kaza.

Kapitulo 15 (Sic. Debería ser el 14)

Kuando Armand saliya dela kaza de Rišard, el era muy alegre. Su konversasyon con Žakomo le aziya kreer ke el iva parvenir a konoser loke el keriya saver. Kon un paso prestozo el se va a kaza, al grande enkanto de su mužer.

"Ke akontesyo, Armand, en medyo del dya, venir en kaza?"

"El menester me ovligo, apunto vengo de resivir un telegrafo de Londra de uno de los mas keridos amigos, Lord Žorž Frodel, kon el kual azemos grandes echos kada mes. El me dize ke partyo de Londra por venir verme, i ke manyana demanyana el estara aki. Esto me ovligo a korer a kaza por dezirte de empesar de agora a azer los aparežos, porke manyana, en vinyendo, el deve komer en kaza."

"Uf! Uf! Uf!..." esklamo la mužer, "no saves komo no me plaze ke vengan musafires en kaza? Partikolarmente kuando es un aženo[174]."

"Ya es verdad, ya saves ke me estoy akavidando mas del karar[175] a no traerte ğente en kaza, ma este Lord, kon el kual ago yo grandes echos, so ovligado de traerlo en kaza."

"Tanto ke mos afita[176], en todo cavzo, yo no puedo azer nada. Prezentate a un grande restaurante, trata kon el las porsyones ke keres para dar a komer alas personas ke te van a venir a vižitar, i eskapame de afidento[177]."

"No ay ninguno ke va venir a vižitar mas ke solo el Lord."

"Sea komo sea, aze loke keres, yo no puedo fatigarme."

"Esto te lo are kon plazir, no te kanses para esto. Ma... para enderechar un poko la mobilya[178] de kaza, kreo ke ya lo vas a azer."

"En echos de kaza no se mesklan los ombres, yo ya se loke ay de azer, el onor tuyo es el miyo."

"Byen, aze loke keres, yo me vo."

I, saludando a su mužer, el la abraso al uzo de kada diya, y se fue.

Kapitulo 16

Kuando Žákomo kedo solo kon Maurice el se empeso a fregar las manos i kon una dulse sonriza el se empeso a burlar de Maurice en dizyendole.

"Vas a ver komo vo reušir! Tu sos pateta y no te saves espažar[179]. "

"No puedes ainda nada avlar si la ves i si no reušes."

"Yo me konosko muy byen i ya tengo visto muncho mundo."

"Amanyana la tadre avlamos enǧuntos."

Eyos empesavan a konversar de aki i de aya i se davan randevu para irsen ala noche al teatro.

Eyos estuvyeron enǧuntos noche entera en lugares de pasatyempo i kon grande dispasensya esperavan venir la demanyana.

Kom grande yogo[180] eyos durmyeron dos oras de koza i se levantaron por tomar el kafe kon leche i esperar a Armand. Este ultimo tambyen no dormiya la noche entera, kon grande dispasensya el espero la manyana, i kuando vido amaneser, apunto se ronǧo ala kaye. Vergwensandose de ir mui temprano, el izo una chika paseada de serka una ora i se fue derechamente ala kaza de Maurice, ǧusto en el momento ke se aviyan levantado de dormir i tomavan el kafe kon leche.

"Bravo, Armand, dišo Maurice, tu esfuegra te kere muncho byen[181]. Ǧusto en el momento ke vamos a tomar el kafe, vyenes de venir. Ya bevites kafe?"

"Ya bevi tres kopas."

"Austa[182] la cuatrina, toma i dimos[183] ke azites."

"Ke vo azer? Le dise a mi mužer ke va venir de Londra Lord Frodel a vižitarme, y si komo tengo munchos echos kon el, vo traerlo a kaza a pransar oy; i eya me aksepto kon plazir. Ke esta la ora?"

Maurice miro la ora i dišo:

"Dyes i medya."

"Esperaremos otra medya ora, tomamos una caroza i nos vamos."

Kapitulo 17

Ya puedeš kreer la dispasensya de Žakomo i de Armand por ver venir la ora alas onze por partir. Armand era mas dezesperado de Žakomo. Enfin la ora dela pared ḥarvava las 11 i Armand, tomando el braso a Ǧákomo, saliyan de la kaza de Maurice. Eyos alkilavan un luksuozo otomobil i se aziyan yevar a kaza.

Žulyeta ya los estava esperando, eya era vestida de un rob de samber[184], kolor roz ke aziya posar[185] su ermozura, i kon una saludada devida a akeas damas de alta aristokrasya, eya resiviya a su marido kon el auspido.

"Vos prezento Madame Armand," deziya el marido de Žulyet en dizyendole a eya tambyen: "El Lord Frodel."

"Me konto venturoso de konozervos, Madame," dišo Žakomo en apretandole la mano.

La prezentasyon echa, pasaron al salon de resepsyon, onde en vista le ofriyan dulsuryas. Despues delas palavras de uzo i de avlas de echos de aki i de aya, pasaron al pranso[186].

Aki, Sr. Armand empesava a azer onores a Žakomo en keryen[d]o azer asentar a su mužer alado de el, ma Žakomo se apresurava a dezirle en el oyido:

"Enfrente de mi asentala."

Armand egzekutiya este dicho, i Žulyeta se asentava enfrente de Žakomo.

La komida era servida kon grande lukso i las botelyas de šampanya ǧogavan polka de mano a mano en bevyendo kada uno ala salud del otro. Armand beviya ala salud del falso Lord Frodel i kuando veniya el turno de Žakomo, el deziya:

"Ke Sinyor Armand no se aravye, vo bever ala salud dela sinyora Žulyeta por ringrasyarla del kalurozo resivo ke vyene de azerme en resivyendome oy en su kaza."

"Yo no ago ke mi dever. El dever de una mužer es de onorar su marido i en mesmo tyempo los amigos de su marido."

"Vos ringrasyo, Madame, una[187] onor ke no la meresko."

En este momento, Armand saliya de la kamareta por ordenar de traer la fruta, i Žakomo kontinuava.

"Vos ǧuro, Madame, ke si yo saviya ke Armand teniya una mužer de una tan rara ermozura, yo uvyere venido aki de seis mezes antes."

Žulyet se sonrio mui livyanamente i entre si eya se dišo.

"I este Lord parese ser de akeos ke konosemos."

Enfin sirvyeron la fruta. Avlaron despues un poko de aki i de aya, i Žakomo kon un tono seryo dišo:

"Armand, ya es tyempo de partir. Tenemos ke mirar munchos echos."

"Si Sinyor, vamos."

Todos los dos se levantaron, i Žákomo, kon una linda reverensya, apreto la mano de Žulyeta en yevandola a sus mušos[188], i se retiro en inklinandose una sigunda ves. I, salyendo ala puerta, entraron de nuevo al otomobil ke los esperava.

Kapitulo 18

Kuando los dos amigos eran en la kaye era Armand ke le demandava:

"Ke tal, Žakomo? Tengo razon de selarme?"

"Muncha. Sos venturozo de tener una mužer de una rara ermozura, i tyenes muncha razon de kerer konoser si es onesta. En todo kavzo yo are todo loke puedo por kontentarte, empesando de manyana, yo ire a vižitar a Žulyet i buškare a echarla ala peška."

El otomobil los traiya de nuevo a la puerta de kaza de Rišard[189]. Armand se iva a su echo i Žakomo entrava a kaza por ver a su amigo. Este ultimo ya lo esperava i kuando lo vido venir, sus ožos se aklararon en demandandole:

"Ke tal, Žakomo? Ke tal topates[190] a Žulyeta?"

"Sarmante[191]! Son mui raras las mužeres ermozas komo esta. Eya me plazyo bastante, i esto siguro ke yo no pedrire el golpe sigun tu lo pedrites."

"Estas palavras las diše yo propyo, kuando Maurice me izo los eložyos, ma kuando yo me topi delantre de eya,yo remarki ke no es una mužer de pueder ǧugar kon eya, i ke es una mužer onesta."

"Vamos a ver!"

"Si tu reušes en este echo te ǧuro ke te va[192] dar un pranso i te vo gastar 2000 frankos."

Žakomo empeso a sonreir en respondyendo:

"Ninguna mužer fuye de mis brasos. Basta ke eya me plazga. Ala noche tambyen esto invitado a komer, i desde manyana vas a empesar a ver loke Žakomo save azer."

Akel diya lo pasaron por aki i por aya los dos amigos enǧuntos, y ala tadre Armand veniya de nuevo por yevar a Žakomo a su kaza. Esta ves el nuevo amorozo de Žulyeta se iva kon otro vestido, otro chapeo, otra kolor de guantes i otra forma de aniyos. Kon este nuevo luso, eya[193] keriya mostrar ala mužer de Armand ke el era bastante riko.

Kuando Armand i Žakomo entraron en kaza, Žulyeta aziya un kalurozo resivo al amigo de su marido, el kual era esto loke esperava, i en apretandole la mano, el no se travava de dezirle:

"Seriya de korason este kalurozo resivo ke me azes?"

Žulyeta lo mirava en la kara, i kon un tono seryoso respondiya:

"Siguramente, los amigos de mi marido son syempre los amigos de kaza."

Entravan al salon, i la konversasyon empezava.

Žakomo no kitava los ožos de Žulyeta, i en munchas okasyones la dama lo remarkava i posava los ožos enbašo en dizyendo entre si:

"I este parese de akea ǧente."

El pranso aprontado, pasaron a komer, i las botelyas de šampanya empesavan a ǧugar polka en la meza.

Aki tambyen Žakomo topava la okasyon de ḥarvar su kopa kon akea de Žulyeta, i en kada ves ke ḥarvavan las kopas, frazes muy delisyozas eran empleadas por Žakomo, por kerer azer entender a Žulyeta ke le aviya plazido.

Enfin, la komida se eskapo[194], i Žakomo invito al marido i ala mužer a venir al teatro, onde una loǧa[195] era alkilada desde el diya.

La invitasyon era akseptada, el otomobil esperava en la puerta, i los tres enǧuntos entravan adyentro.

Sigun la korteziya egziže, Armand era ovligado de asentar a Žakomo alado de su mužer, i el meterse enfrente.

Esto tambyen era una okasyon a Žakomo por desbafar[196]. Apenas el se asentava alado de Žulyeta, ke el le deziya a bos baša en el oyido:

"Madame, kuanto so venturoso de tenervos a mi lado."

Žulyeta no respondiya, i Žakomo empesava a sospechar en dizyendo entre si:

"Este gweso parese ke va salir muy duro."

Enfin arivavan al teatro.

En *mazal* bueno de Armand, akea noche ǧugavan la pyesa entitulada "El selozo". Era una pyesa onde mostrava ke un marido ke amava muncho a su mužer, la selava muncho, la guadrava muncho, i anke la adorava, syempre saliya plyetos[197] en kaza a kavza del selo.

No tenyendo kriaturas, la mužer se enfastyava de su marido, i se fuiya en dešandolo.

Esta pyesa traia grande batimento de korason a Armand. Ma le dava tambyen una grande arma a Žakomo para pueder empesar a avlar en estos terminos:

"Ke tal topaš esta pyesa, Madame? Ken tyene razon, el marido o la mužer?"

"Ni el marido, ni la mužer. Porke un marido es seloso, una mužer no deve vender su onor, el solo kapital ke una mužer deve tener en la familya."

Esta repuesta no konveniya a Žakomo, ma el no deviya nada azer. El deviya kayarse por akel momento.

Enfin, el teatro se eskapo. Armand i Žulyet se fueron a kaza i Žakomo iva al otel por echarse.

171

Kapitulo 19

Kuando Žakomo se espartyo[198] de Armand i Žulyet, el se fue al otel i, echandose al lecho, el empeso a pensar loke el deviya azer por reušir en loke el keriya. El topava el gweso muy duro, i empesava a dar razon a Rišard. Akea noche, el no durmyo noche entera i, a la manyana, apunto ke se levanto, el dyo una dada ensima dela meza en dizyendo:

"No ay remedyo... el empesižo[199] de toda sorte de echo es fuerte, ma a mizura ke se empesa ya kamina despues."

El se viste, sale ala kaye, toma el café kon leche, se arapa, i espera kon dispasensya en un kafe el arivo delas oras dyes y medya. Kuando el ve la ora dela pared ḥarvar las dyes el se levanta i empesa a kaminar con pasos vagarozos.[200] Ǧusto alas dyes y medya Žákomo es delantre la puerta dela kaza de Armand. El ḥarva la puerta, el moso le avre, lo konose en vista i lo invita a entrar.

"Sinyor Armand esta en kaza?" demanda el.

"No Sinyor."

"I Madame?"

"Madame se esta vistyendo i va salir ala kaye."

"Vos rogo informarla de mi vižita."

El moso se va, i retorna en dizyendo ke le es imposivle de resivir ente en kaza kuando su marido no esta.

"En todo kavzo, una ves ke veniteš a buškar al Sinyor Armand, Madame dišo ke puedeš venir [a] la ora del pranso a toparlo."

Ya puedeš kreer la temblor de alma del žoven amorozo ke se deziya entre si:

"Rišard fue mas *mazalozo*[201] de mi. Akel tuvo la ventura de ser resivido una o dos vezes en kaza, sin estar el marido, myentras ke yo no tuve ni esta šans[202]. El pensava ansi en el kortižo, kuando subito Žulyeta abašava la eskalera vestida i kon chapeo en la kavesa por salir ala

172

kaye. Remarkando a Žákomo enpyes en el kortižo i pensativle, eya se sonrio i le dišo:"

"Eskuzadme, Sinyor Lord, si no vos resivi. Yo esto muy presada[203] por ir onde una amiga, ala kual di randevu alas oras onze i no manka ke kinze puntos."

"Teneš razon, Madame, ma... keriya avlarvos de un echo impor..."

"Ya se de kualo me vaš a avlar, i la verdad dezirvos es ǧustamente por esto ke no vos resivi."

"Kualo puedeš saver sin ke yo vos diga nada?"

"No ay menester de avlar, Sinyor Lord. Vuestras miradas de ayer enel pranso i de anoche enel teatro ya bastan para entender loke vos kereš dezir. En todo kavzo no pyedraš vuestro tyempo en vanidades. Yo no so de akeas bravas mužeres ke vos konoseš, ke saven austar el budǧeto[204] kon regalos de amigos. Yo devo tener un amigo solo en la vida, i este ya lo tengo. El es mi marido."

"Ma Madame, estaš endo[205] muy lešos, antes ke yo tengo la ozadiya de avlar."

"No ay menester de avlar, ya entendi todo."

Žakomo iva kontinuar a avlar, ma Žulyeta no le dešo el tyempo. Eya lo dešo kon la palavra en la boka i salyo de kaza. El otomobil ya estava esperandola, eya entro adyentro e indiko al sofur[206] onde eya se deviya ir.

Žakomo kedava enpyes komo aro sin aza[207], komo dizen las mužeres. El empesava a pensar i subito el esklamava.

"Yo me vo ir onde el marido. Vo venir kon el a komer, le va[208] dezir a su marido.

Entrega 7

ke salga de kaza sin avertir a su mužer, i veremos loke el va azer despues."

El sale dela kaza de Armand i se va derechamente ala kamareta de ofisyo[209] de Armand. El lo topa eskrivyendo, i kon un bonǧorno de kara de riza se aserka de el en espandyendole la mano.

"Oh! Bonğorno, esklama Armand, "seas byen venido. Ke ay de nuevo?"

"Nada. Tu mužer no me kižo resivir anke insisti a konversar kon eya. Eya dišo ke era muy okupada i dešandome kon la palavra en la boka, se fue a azer una vižita i me dešo empyes en la puerta dela kaye en dizyendome:"

"Si kereš konversar kon me, venid a mezoğorno kon mi marido en ğuntos[210]."

"Esto no esta bueno," esklamo Armand. "Delantre de mi no vas a pueder nada avlar."

"Es verdad, ma me pensi otra koza. Este mezo ğorno[211] iremos enğuntos en kaza i, apenas eskapas de komer, te fuyes de kaza sin darle avizo i, kuando yo sere solo kon eya, yo savre muy byen ğugar mi rolo[212]."

"I esta idea es buena!" Armand mira la ora, i vyendo ke ya esta kaži onze i medya, el dize.

"Vamos de agora, tendras medya ora demaziya para konversar kon mi mužer, i esto te ara mas muncho familyarizar."

"Mas tu mužer no esta ainda en kaza. Eya dižo ke teniya randevu kon una amiga alas oras 11 i ay apenas medya ora ke se fue."

"No importa. Vamos. Puede ser la topano[213]. Saves tu, mi mužer es mui fina[214]. Es mui posivle ke en sintyendo ke tu venites a vižitarla, se vistyo ekspresamente por mostrar ke va salir, i ritorno despues. Vamos,vas a ver komo tengo razon."

Eyos saliyan afuera, tomaron un otomobil i se aziyan yevar a kaza.

Kapitulo 20

Esta ves Armand se aviya yerado en su ğuzgamyento. Žulyeta ya se aviya ido a vižitar onde una amiga yamada Madame Klotild, una vyeža amiga de la eskola ke se amavan muncho. Madame Klotild le aziya un kalurozo resivo i topava ke Žulyet estava muy pensativle i tokada de kolor.

"Kerida Žulyet, ke tyenes? demando Klotild."

"No se ni yo loke tengo. Bivo muy venturoza kon el solo regreto ke mi marido es selozo."

"Todos los maridos son selozos."

"Ma no es komo el miyo. Este mizeravle esta metyendo personas para ver si yo lo vo enganyar. I la persona es kuero y gweso. Del diya ke kazi, ya son kuatro o sinco personas ke metyo para ke me enganyen. A todos ya les refuzi ma, el Dyo guadre, un gwerko me puede rovar el korason i, la verdad dezirte, no kero enganyar a mi marido."

"Sos bova, a semežantes maridos kale enganyar mas presto."

"No, kerida, el onor antes de todo. Esto prenyada i no kero ke mi kriatura no sea iža[215] de su padre."

"Alora, kale ke buskes a konvenserlo ke esta yerado."

"Ya le avli munchas vezes. El no kere entender."

Apenas Žulyet pronunsiava esta ultima fraze ke una idea le veniya al tino i eya esklamava:

"Ya topi! Te ğuro, Klotild, ke le vo dar una buena leisyon[216], vas a ver."

Las dos amigas empesaron a konversar de aki i de aya, i ğusto alas oras 12 menos 10 puntos, Žulyet saludava a su amiga i se retirava. El otomobil ya estava esperandola en la puerta. I ğusto a las oras 12 la mužer de Armand ya era en su kaza. Eya no se enkantava del todo de ver a Žakomo en su kaza akompanyado de su marido.

"Sea byen venido, Sinyor Žakomo, sustuviteš vuestra palavra, agora, delantre de mi marido, puedeš avlar todo

175

loke kereš."

Žakomo se aziya kolorado por mostrar ke no era delantre de su marido ke la konversasyon deviya tener lugar. El echo los ožos enbašo, i kon los musos izo senyas a Žulyet de no avlar delantre su marido.

La mužer de Armand se sonrio en ronğandole una mirada de akeas ke arankan un pedaso del korason.

El pranso era pronto i todos los tres pasaron en vista a komer.

La primera komida trayida era la sopa.

"Una nueva sopa ya se kome[217]," dižo Žakomo, "bendicha mano ke tal la izo. "

La sigunda komida ke serviyan era la gaina[218]. Žulyet eskodyava[219] eya mesma a todos los dos, i buskava ekspresamente a tomarse para eya la partida onde ay el *yades*[220]. Esto echo, empesaron a komer i kuando vino el gweseziko del *yades* a la mano de Žulyet esta ultima dišo a su marido.

"Armand, keres meter *yades*?[221]"

"A kualo?"

"O me merkas un *fostanlik*[222] o te merko un pardesu[223]."

"De akordo."

I marido i mužer rompian el *yades*.

Traian despues aros i komposto[224], i Armand apenas eskapava de komer, topava una okasyon ke su mužer estava por aki por aya i se fuiya en dešando a Žakomo solo en kaza.

Kapitulo 21

Ya puedeš kreer la alegriya de Žakomo en vyendose solo en kaza ğuntos kon Žulyeta. Esta ultima, no savyendo ke su marido ya aviya partido, veniya asentarse de nuevo al deredor dela meza, i vyendo solo a Žakomo, kreyo ke su marido se aviya ido a lavarse la boka, i eya se asento komo antes enfrente del el.

Žakomo se empesava a fregar las manos en tomando la palavra.

"Madame, sigun lo veš, no manki de egzekutir vuestros[225] ordenes i vine ğuntos kon vuestro marido. Agora ke el no esta prezente aki, kereš darme la otorisasyon de avlarvos algunos byervos?"

Žulyeta miro kon atansyon a Žakomo i le demando en sonriyendo.

"Vos rogo ke me digaš, i a vos, vos enkargo mi marido porke proveš mi onestidad?"

"Madame, vos ğuro ke inyoro de todo loke me estaš avlando."

"Alora, kualo es loke kereš avlar con mi?"

"Demandar vuestra pyedad, Madame. Del primer momento ke vos enkontri, no se ke tengo, Madame, mi korason me bate, mi alma se kere despedasar, i a verdad dezirvos, Madame, anke tengo frekuentado munchas mužeres, es por la primera ves ke empeso a entender loke es amor."

"Estaš repitando las mesmas palavras ke todos los ombres dizen kuando keren echar ala peska a alguna mužer."

"Vos ğuro ke no, Madame, tened pyedad de mi. Un rifuso de vuestra parte sera kondanarme a la muerte."

Žulyeta empesava a pensar i Žakomo kontinuava.

"Madame, vos rogo, vos supliko, tened konfianza en mi. Yo vos amo!"

I en dizyendo estos byervos Žakomo se echava a

ğinolyos[226] delantre la mužer de Armand en kontinuando:"

"Madame, tened pyedad.

Žulyeta levantava de enbašo a Žakomo en dizyendole:

"Los ombres son tan falsos ke no se puede kreer mesmo
a akeos ke avlan la verdad. Vuestra fizyonomiya me
plazyo bastante, ma me espanto no sea un espyon de mi
marido."

"Madame, vos estaš yerando. Vos ğuro por loke tengo
de mas sacro en la vida ke vos amo de puro korason i no
ay ningun espyonaže enmedyo. Ala kontra, si akseptaš a
kitar[227] a vuestro marido, esto pronto a azervos mi mužer,
en prometyendovos de azervos gozar de una vida unika
en la vida."

"Byen, dešadme pensar asta manyana ala medyo diya.
Venid a komer aki kon mi marido komo lo aziteš oy, ala
sola kondisyon ke apenas eskapaš de komer vos vaš a ale-
vantar por partir. Si me desidi a amarvos, vos vo
akompanyar asta el kortižo i vos vo guadrar en un
almaryo del kortižo fin ke parte mi marido. Si viteš ke no
vos akompanyi es ke no tengo idea de amarvos, i no vos
amrivaš[228] mas a venir por mi kaza."

"Ma, Madame, vos rogo de darme un poko de esperansa."

"Kontad mas por una repuesta afirmativa ke negativa."

"Vos ringrasyo, Madame, dinyad darme un akonto[229] a
mi amor por vos, Madame."

"Por oy nada, no vos vo saludar ni kon la mano. Es muy
posivle ke mi marido se eskondyo en algun kanton[230] por
ver nuestra konversasyon."

Žakomo se levanto en vista i kon grande difikultad
pudo apanyar la mano de Žulyet i yevarsela a los musos.

El se retiro, kontente de aver arivado al primer paso de
su reušita.

"Yo no vo avlar nada a Armand," deziya el entre si,
"porke si yo parveni a enganyar a Žulyet, sera un plan
para kada diya i no es ğusto ke lo sepa su marido."

El abaso[231] al kortižo kon grande alegriya i empeso a

178

mirar onde aviya algun almaryo.

Subito Armand se le aparesyo delantre en demandandole:

"Ke izites, Žakomo?"

"Nada, tu mužer es onesta. En todo kavzo vo a venir amanyana a komer a tu kaza, si reuši, byen. Tanto[232] ke no, kere dezir ke no ay mas onesta de tu mužer."

De esta manera, Žakomo enganyava a su amigo, i esperava kon grande despasensya el arivo del diya sigyente.

Enfin, el diya sigyente arivava, i Žakomo veniya de nuevo a komer ala kaza de Žulyeta akompanyado de su marido.

La patrona de kaza le aziya un kalurozo resivo, i mas ke syempre eya le mostrava kara alegre, por azerle entender ke ya estava de akordo sovre la konversasyon del diya de antes.

Kon los ožos Žakomo demandava a Žulyeta si aviya una repuesta favoravle, i Žulyeta respondiya kon las sežas[233] una repuesta afirmava[234], repuesta ke aziya muncho alegrar al sinyor musafir.

La komida terminada, Žakomo se levantava por saludar. Žulyeta lo akompanyava asta el kortižo i, avryendo un grande gard rob[235], lo aziya entrar adyentro en serando la puerta kon yave i retornava alado de su marido komo si nada no[236] uvyera akontesido.

Armand de su parte se aparežava a partir ma su mužer lo deteniya dizyendole:

"Asenta, Armand, tengo menester de avlar un poko con ti."

"Ma yo tengo mis echos, ke sea ala noche."

"No, Armand, oy propyo[237] kero ke me digas ke va ser el kavo de este komporto tuyo. Vas metyendo a uno i a otro para ke me proven, sin pensar ke un diya, alguno me puede plazir i me puede enganyar."

"Yo no meti a ninguno para ke buske a enganyarte."

"Mentiras! Tu metites a munchos, i en ultimo lugar a Žakomo."

"A Žakomo?! A Žakomo meti yo para ke te prove?"

"Si. La prova es ke sin dezirte nada, el me izo la

deklarasyon de amor i me dišo ke si yo lo kontentava me iva deskuvrir un sekreto."

"I tu ke izites?"

"La verdad ke te diga, Armand, a todos rifuzi sus proposisyon, ma a Žakomo no pude. El me harvo en el alma, i yo lo prometi ke oy lo va[238] kontentar."

"Oy lo vas a kontentar?!... Despues ke me vo ir yo?"

"Ǧustamente."

"Žakomo va venir de nuevo aki?"

"Ya esta aki, no ay menester de venir."

"Onde esta el?"

"Yo lo guadri en el gard rob del kortižo."

Armand se metiya en kolora en esklamando entre si:

"El mizeravle, va enganyar a mi mužer sin darme avizo. I alsando su bos el kontinuo en koryendo al kortižo:

"Yo matare a este miseravle!"

"Ke estas koryendo?" esklamo su mužer, "La yave del almaryo la tengo yo. Komo vas a avrir?"

I la mužer le da la yave, ma apenas el marido la toma ke eya esklamma[239]:

"Yades! Te gani! Ma no solo el *fustan*, ma tambyen el sospecho ke teniyas por mi. Si yo keriya guadrar el namorado, na ke lo supe guadrar delantre de ti, la ora ke tu no sospecharas. En todo kavzo, por asigurarte, va avre el almaryo i lo toparas adyentro."

Armand se fue, i a su grande enkanto[240] topo a Žakomo enel gard rob, el kual se enkantava tambyen de ver ke Armand avriya el almaryo en lugar de Žulyet, ke se esperava.

Esta leisyon basto a Sinyor Armand a no selarse mas, i Sinyor Žakomo retorno a su kamareta kon los mokos enkolgando, ǧugado por akea mužer ke el keriya ǧugar.

Desde este diya, marido i mužer bivyeron muy kontentes, i en la ora mižor kuando topavan un yades en la gaina Armand se espantava de meter yades, akodrandose del fustan i del musafir del almaryo.

FIN

Demandad Todos el Romanso

La Kunyada
Sin Korason

1 En vista: en seguida.
2 Musafir (turco): invitado.
3 Bavažadas; tonterías.
4 *Amistad* en esta novela significa *amor*.
5 Negras: malas.
6 ğelvi (turco): forma de hablar de una mujer para captar a un hombre.
7 Ağiğaš: le tenéis lástima.
8 Gwerko: diablo.
9 *Sus* en vez de *su* de acuerdo con el plural precedente *mužeres*.
10 Buto (francés *but*): finalidad.
11 (buena) suerte (hebreo *mazal*, lit. *planeta*).
12 *supe:* sospecha.
13 *puša*: empuja.
14 *kale*: es preciso.
15 *Echo*: asunto, ocupación, negocio.
16 Sic en el texto.
17 Sic en el texto.
18 Sic en el texto.
19 Turko: complacencia.
20 Tienda (francés *magasin)*.
21 Sorpresa.
22 Ortografiado *samej, yod* más una apóstrofe.
23 "Flos" o "Fluss". Este apellido asquenasí correspondería a los apellidos no-sefardíes que el autor da a Armand y Žulyeta.
24 Puntos: minutos.
25 Debe ser "saver". El impresor repitió la *samej* de "deves".
26 juntos sic.
27 Ğaailik (turco): negligencia, descuido, comportamiento infantil. Aquí debe significar comportamiento irresponsable.
28 Conocer sexualmente a muchas mujeres.
29 Recibir (francés *recevoir)*.
30 Sólo (francés *ne... que)*.
31 Amabilidad.
32 Sic en el texto. Bebe ser sos.
33 Sic en el texto.
34 seducir (turco *sombair*).
35 Sic en el texto.
36 Precisamente (francés *justement)*.
37 Fósforo (turco *kyevrit*).
38 Enciende.
39 Acostumbrada.
40 Dar y recibir.
41 Echar de la casa, rechazar.

⁴² Pransar (italiano *pranzo):* (comer).

⁴³ Sic en el texto.

⁴⁴ *pyango* (turco) lotería (habrán acertado).

⁴⁵ Es decir, que no lo revele.

⁴⁶ Tener éxito (francés *réussir).* A veces Karmona lo escribe o el impresor lo imprime sin diacrítica en la letra *shin.*

⁴⁷ Debes...

⁴⁸ Sombrero (portugués *chapéu).*

⁴⁹ *Afrito:* dolor.

⁵⁰ prohibir (francés *défendre).*

⁵¹ huésped.

⁵² sorprender.

⁵³ La palabra termina con la letra *mem,* pero creemos mejor poner *Madame* i no el inglés *Madam,* ya que con gran probabilidad se decía la palabra con la fonética francesa.

⁵⁴ Agradezco.

⁵⁵ De ninguna manera (francés *du tout):*

⁵⁶ Gran deseo.

⁵⁷ pero (italiano *ma).*

⁵⁸ La letra ḥ representa aquí la letra gutural hebrea *het.*

⁵⁹ Sic. Quizás debería de ser "me izo".

⁶⁰ Turco: apasionarse.

⁶¹ Sic. Debe ser em.

⁶² Empujado.

⁶³ loco.

⁶⁴ Sic ¿debe ser "no sabe"?

⁶⁵ "acabava de" (francés *venait de).*

⁶⁶ Suerte (francés *chance).*

⁶⁷ Escrito con dos letras *reš.*

⁶⁸ "amigo mío" (francés *mon cher).*

⁶⁹ Normalmente *por tanto* en judeo-español traduce el francés *pourtant:* ("sin embargo" en castellano). Aquí parece que significa lo mismo que "por lo tanto" en castellano moderno.

⁷⁰ Sic en el texto.

⁷¹ Yendo.

⁷² *Oler la boka:* buscar enterarse lo que piensa una persona acerca de algo.

⁷³ "escandalizada" o "maravillada".

⁷⁴ *Enfastiyar:* enfadar; aburrir.

⁷⁵ Destinada.

⁷⁶ *Fišugar:* importunar.

⁷⁷ Sic.

⁷⁸ Sic, con inflexión femenina.

⁷⁹ Sic.

⁸⁰ Juramentos.

81 mediodía (italiano *mezzogiorno)*:
82 *Ǧoliya*: joyas.
83 *Beke:* celador de noche (turco b*ekdje*).
84 *No lo embezamos*: lo aprendemos.
85 Sic.
86 *kavakar:* hurgar, revelando lo que hubiera quedado mejor escondido.
87 La entrega termina en medio de la palabra.
88 Decidir.
89 lograr (francés *parvenir*).
90 *boš bogas:* tonto, indiscreto (turco.cuello vacío).
91 Insistiendo, como si fuera con un martillo.
92 Sic.
93 dinero (turco p*aras*).
94 *Eskaparsen*: Acabarlos.
95 *Enfastyado*: cansado.
96 metres querida (francés *maîtresse*).
97 *ḥazinura*: enfermedad.
98 Sic, pero sigue siendo poco claro. ¿Quiere decir "tu estas puedyendo alcansar"?
99 He aquí (turco *Na*).
100 *Embezar*: enseñar.
101 Terminación estilo castellano que remata el verbo francés.
102 Sic. *Buškar una alguža en un pajar* es no encontrar lo que se busca y, por extensión, buscar lo que ya se lleva mucho tiempo buscando sin éxito porque es imposible.
103 Sic. ¿Debería der "esperando"?
104 Sic, con la "me" enclítica separada del verbo anterior.
105 *Fyere*: hiere.
106 Sic, en femenino.
107 Puntuación sic.
108 aun (francés *même*).
109 *Kitaldo*: Quitadlo.
110 Sillón (francés *fauteui*).
111 Sic por "komunikarvos".
112 se hicieron (francés *devenir* con inflexión castellana).
113 *ḥazinos*: enfermos.
114 Sic.
115 Una teoría sobre la naturaleza de los hijos de adulterio. No menciona el autor que tales hijos son *mamzerim*, los cuales el derecho matrimonial judío prohibe que se casen excepto con otros como ellos.
116 Sic.
117 Sic.
118 Riesgo.

119 *karar*: determinación, cantidad.
120 solucionar una dificultad en la que uno está metido (francés *débrouiller*).
121 Guio. La letra gimmel sin marca diacrítica se pronuncia dura.
122 desafortunadamente (francés *malheureusement*).
123 Sic.
124 collar (francés *collier*).
125 Sic en singular.
126 Sic. Vista la segunda frase, quizás debería ser "NO tyenes razón..."
127 Se separan.
128 joyero (francés *bijoutier*).
129 ejemplos.
130 opcionalmente (turco *muhayyer*).
131 Adivinar que el marido tiene que ser responsable de la visita de Maurice.
132 Sic por *kolera*.
133 Sic.
134 *San Pablo* (¿?) en el sentido de "hijo de vecino".
135 Sic, por *azeš*
136 Arteros.
137 Sic, "va' en vez de "vo".
138 Ibid.
139 Cita (francés *rendezvous*).
140 Acaba de (francés *vient de*).
141 Sofá (francés *canapé*).
142 Buenas tardes (francés *bonsoir*).
143 Oye.
144 Picar.
145 Vehemente.
146 Sic. Quizás significa "*al cabo*".
147 Se afeita.
148 Fría.
149 Esperar en vano.
150 Es decir, *misercordiosas*.
151 Sic. Es corriente el uso del plural *sus* con sustantivo singular, quizás por influencia del francés *leur*.
152 En algunos casos hemos insertado la diacrítica cuando parece que el cajista la ha omitido por accidente, como en el caso de *teneš*.
153 Tema (francés *sujet*).
154 Sic. Debería ser *ovligada*.
155 ¿Debería ser *kontentar*?
156 Sin embargo (francés *pourtant*).

185

[157] *Remordimiento* (francés *remords*).
[158] *Cabizbajo.*
[159] Profundo pensamiento.
[160] Preocupado (francés *troublé*).
[161] Sic con letra b.
[162] ¿Significa "protesté"?
[163] Es decir, *yo te voy a.*
[164] Cesta.
[165] Hesitar.
[166] Capaz.
[167] Se dirigió.
[168] Sólo (francés *ne..que*).
[169] Sic. plural.
[170] Deseaba (francés *désirait*).
[171] Después son 500.
[172] Sic aunque después se ortografía *kapachidad*.
[173] Ya (francés *déjà*).
[174] extranjero o quizás no-judío.
[175] haciendo más de lo que es necesario.
[176] ya que nos toca.
[177] libérame de la obligación.
[178] Muebles.
[179] *Pateta* = pesado. *Espažar* = meter fin a un tema.
[180] ¿placer?
[181] *Esfuegra*: Suegra. Significa que una persona ha venido por casualidad en el momento justo.
[182] Completar (italiano *aggiustar*).
[183] Dinos.
[184] bata (francés *robe de chambre).*
[185] ¿destacar?
[186] Da la impresión que se comía a mediodía, sea por ser lo normal, sea porque esa hora es la francesa.
[187] sic en femenino.
[188] labios.
[189] En el capítulo anterior se trataba de la casa de Maurice.
[190] ¿Qué tal de parece? (francés *Comment as-tu trouvé Juliette?*).
[191] encantadora (francés *charmante).* No hay diacrítica en la ese.
[192] Sic.
[193] Sic. Debería ser *el.*
[194] acabó.
[195] palco (francés *loge).*
[196] Expresar sus opiniones.
[197] peleas.
[198] se separó.

199 comienzo.

200 ¿Debería ser *vigorozos*?

201 afortunado (hebreo *mazal* con teminación adjetival castellano).

202 suerte (francés *chance*).

203 tengo prisa (francés *pressée*).

204 presupuesto (francés *budget*).

205 Sic. Quizás debería de empezar con *lamed yod* y no *alef yod*.

206 chófer (francés *chauffeur*).

207 jarro sin asa.

208 Sic.

209 despacho.

210 Sic, en dos palabras.

211 Sic, en dos palabras.

212 papel (francés *rôle*).

213 Sic. ¿Debería ser *la topamos*?

214 Inteligente.

215 Sic en femenino.

216 Sic. La palabra es ortografiada *lamed-yod-alef-yod-samej-yod-yod- vav-nun*.

217 Sic

218 *Gaina*: gallina.

219 *Eskodyar*: apartar, servir.

220 *Yades* (turco): el hueso de la suerte.

221 Meter yades: cuando uno tiene que pagar una prenda si toma algo de la mano del otro sin gritar "yades!"

222 vestido (turco).

223 abrigo (francés *pardessus*).

224 fruta hervida (francés *compôte*).

225 sic. masculino.

226 rodillas.

227 dejar (francés *quitter*).

228 no te atrevas.

229 anticipo.

230 rincón.

231 sic. ¿debía de ser *bašo al kortižo*?

232 mientras.

233 cejas.

234 Sic por *afirmativa*.

235 armario (francés *garderobe*).

236 no... nada (francés *rien... ne*).

237 Mismo.

238 Sic.

239 Sic con dos *mem*.

240 Sorpresa.